The Improbable
Casebook
of Sherlock Holmes

By Nick Cardillo

Hardcover ISBN 978-1-78705-877-4
Paperback ISBN 978-1-78705-878-1
ePub ISBN 978-1-78705-879-8
PDF ISBN 978-1-78705-880-4

Published in the UK by MX Publishing
335 Princess Park Manor, Royal Drive,
London, N11 3GX
www.mxpublishing.co.uk

Cover design by Brian Belanger

Table of Contents

Dr. Watson's Introduction   3

The Scholar of Silchester Court   6

The Adventure of the Deadly Inheritance   45

The Giant Rat of Sumatra   79

A Ghost from the Past   119

The Adventure of the Weeping Stone   157

Death in the House of the Black Madonna   195

In the Footsteps of Madness   244

Acknowledgements   283

About the Author   285

Dr. Watson's Introduction

Mr. Sherlock Holmes was always fond of reminding me that once the impossible has been eliminated, whatever remains regardless of the improbability – must be the truth. It was one of the detective's guiding tenants whenever he faced a problem of indescribable complexity.

These words ring out loudly now as I prepare the following manuscript; an account of several adventures which I undertook at Holmes' side. Each of the problems presented herein are some of the most fantastic chapters in my association with the Great Detective. Should you, my reading public, find these cases impossible to comprehend, I wish to offer you a word of friendly warning.

As Holmes' friend and chronicler during even his most delicate of investigations, I was sometimes forced to alter names and dates in an effort to spare the public undue hardship and, in some cases, protect parties whose reputation – or very lives – could be threatened by the publication of my work.

In this instance, however, I can assure you that no changes have been made to this manuscript. The tales included within these pages appear just as they occurred. They may seem improbable, but you have my word that they are all true.

John H. Watson, M.D.

London, 1925

The Scholar of Silchester Court

Originally Published in The MX Book of New Sherlock
Holmes Stories: Part XIX

In glancing over the notes which I have kept of my time with
Mr. Sherlock Holmes, I am always awed by the detective's
ability to remain ever the rationalist, ever the cold, calculating
machine who never once let the follies of the unexplained
weigh upon him. To a man of lesser stuff than my companion,
he might have been led astray; influenced by the unexplained
and seemingly unexplainable, and ultimately come up with a
solution which simply had no accord in the real world. In
times of reflection, I wonder if I had never met Holmes and,
if I were on my own in some of the situations which we found
ourselves, if my resolve should have been diminished.

As I flip through the pages of my notebooks, several
such cases immediately present themselves as fine examples
of Holmes' maxim that the world was big enough for us; that
no ghosts need apply. There was, of course, the affair of
Robert Ferguson and his son; the infamous tale on the Cornish
Coast; and I should be remiss if I did not put down mention of

the Baskerville family. All of these cases I have deemed it appropriate for the reading public at large to read, but there were many, many instances in which my friend stared the impossible in the face and denounced it. Matters such as the curious case of the absent headmaster and the incredible affair of the lady in the jade kimono naturally present themselves, as do the unusual circumstances surrounding Mr. Larkin, the scholar of Silchester Court.

It was in the early days of my acquaintance with Sherlock Holmes; a chilly autumn morning on the brink of winter. It was a quiet morning as Holmes and I busied ourselves with the routine: I seated by the fire with the first edition of *The Times*, while Holmes sat before his chemical apparatus making detailed notes in the margins of one of his innumerable reference volumes. We sat in silence like this for nearly an hour before I heard Holmes' voice cut through the quiet which had enveloped us:

"You have decided against a brisk stroll, then, Watson?"

I cast a glance over to my friend who was peering down the lens of a microscope. "I beg your pardon?"

Without lifting his gaze from his specimen, Holmes continued. "You had intimated some time ago that you were keen on a walk about town. I believe you even asked me if I were interested in accompanying you, but you know my distaste for exercise for the sake of exercise alone. If you had handled me a foil and instructed me to duel you here in our very rooms, I should have been more keen for I would, at least, be grooming my swordsmanship skills. But I digress.

"Nonetheless, on account of the rain you have foregone this desire; your boots, however, remaining unvarnished and uncleaned in the event that when the rain dissipates you should lace them up anew and head off on your sojourn. We have had a stretch of four clear days now, and this morning you put your boots out to be cleaned, suggesting to me that you have no wishes of strutting about any more lest you scuff them entirely."

"Your train of reasoning is exact in every regard," I replied. "And it is so simple."

Holmes lifted his eyes from the microscope and stared at me from across the room. "Everything, when explained away, is rendered absurdly simple. It is the presentation of a conclusion without the initial inference linked up to it that produces such an astonishing affect."

Holmes stood from the stool before his workbench and thrust his hands deep into the pockets of his tattered, mouse-colored dressing gown which bore many stains and marks from years of arrant cigarette ash and chemical experimentation. He plucked up his preferred pipe from the mantelpiece and applied a match to the bowl. "The world in which we live," he continued as he began to pace up and down before the fire, "is actually a simple one. Despite what Hamlet may have told Horatio, there is not more on heaven and earth than can be dreamed of, studied, and calculated. Much like the work of the actor or the conjurer, it is the work of the ingenious criminal to suggest that there is more than what our eyes see or our ears hear. As a detective, I have trained myself to peer beyond the veil which obscures and complicates the truth."

I cast aside the paper and stood to gather up my own pipe from where I had laid it on the breakfast table. As I began to lazily fill it, I cast a glance out the window and perceived the figure of a man pacing back and forth on the pavement before our door.

"I say, Holmes, I rather think that you have a client."

We both moved to the bay window and looked down into the street below. Indeed, there was a man, dressed in a rather shabby tweed suit who moved with trepidatious steps across the causeway; stopping every so often to cast an imploring glance up at our windows and then continue traversing his stunted path.

Holmes suddenly threw open the window and called down into the street:

"Sir! If you seek my assistance, I do invent you in. If you touch the bell there, my housekeeper shall be more than inclined to show you up."

Then refastening the window, my friend turned to me with a smug smile.

"I do hope that that shall help the poor fellow to make up his mind," he declared. A moment later, the bell was ringing from below and another moment later, the man himself was in our sitting room. As I looked at him now, I became keenly aware of the man's learned features and he seemed to contemplate both Holmes and I through the eyes of an intellectual. There was, however, a queer sense of anxiety that hung over the man. He clasped his hands together as he stepped into our room; the thumb driving into the palm of the other.

"Mr. Sherlock Holmes," he said in a tentative voice; thin and reedy.

"I am Mr. Holmes," my friend replied, "and this is my colleague, Dr. Watson. Please, have a seat, Mr. –"

"Larkin," our visitor said, slowly lowering himself into the chair proffered for our guest, "Augustus Larkin."

Holmes slid into his own chair before the fire and pulled on his pipe. "Larkin," he said contemplatively, "no relation to the scholar, surely?"

"No," Larkin said. "Sylvester Larkin was my father. An academic of the classics, Mr. Holmes. But you seem already familiar with his work."

"Your father's treatise on the role of Salarino in *The Merchant of Venice* is an invaluable piece of research to any actor or historian, for that matter." Holmes pointed with the stem of his pipe. "I perceive ink upon your own fingers, Mr. Larkin. Have you followed your father's footsteps into academia?"

"Indeed, I have," Larkin replied, "but I fear that I have not had such successes as my father. I have had a few, minor speaking engagements, but my academic works have not been met with as much praise as my late father's. The works of a folklorist seldom do, I am afraid."

"Folklore?" I asked. "That is your area of study?"

"Yes," Larkin answered. "English folklore has always been an area of intense interest for me. Even as a boy when my father would read to me the classics, and pry apart the words of *Macbeth*, I did not much care for the literary intricacies over which he obsessed. I simply wanted to know more about the witches. I endeavored to learn much more, and in time I did. I have been fortunate enough to publish a few papers in esteemed journals, but the works have not been able to keep me afloat. I have had to take on several jobs in order to make ends meet. However, of late, I find myself driven completely to distraction unable to concentrate upon anything."

"What is worrying you so, Mr. Larkin? It does not take a detective to tell that you were clearly perturbed."

Larkin drew in a deep breath. "Would you think me mad, Mr. Holmes, if I told you that for the past three weeks, I have been able to predict the future?"

For an instant, it felt as if all the air had been sucked out of the room. The silence which had descended over Holmes and I that morning had returned only with even greater weight.

"I do not even need to hear your answer to know what it is," Larkin said. "Surely, the notion of predicting the future is absurd. Yet, I cannot deny what has been happening to me, gentlemen. I wake from my sleep feeling not refreshed but more drained, for I hear the voices from another world and they warn me of the things that are to come."

"Perhaps," said Holmes, leaning back in his seat, "you had best start your tale from the beginning. Omit nothing, no matter how insignificant you may think it."

Holmes closed his eyes and pressed his palms together under his chin in his usual stance of contemplation. I reached for my notebook and began to take notes as Larkin started to speak.

"I suppose the only place to start is with the place itself: Silchester Court. I cannot imagine that you have heard the name, Mr. Holmes, let alone the history that is connected up to it, so allow me to elucidate for a moment. Silchester Court is, today, a cheap tenement in Soho. It is mostly inhabited by some of this city's less fortunate residents. Conditions are hardly ideal, but it is a haven for those of us at low water. For me, the place comes with something of greater interest: history. You see, centuries ago, Silchester Court was the seat of the Silchester family; a wealthy banking family in the seventeenth century. The patriarch of the Silchester clan was Elias Silchester who, it was believed, from contemporaries, was capable of communicating with the dead. Some of Silchester's more envious business rivals accused Silchester of being a fraud, yet he maintained his clairvoyance to the end. In his own diary, Silchester wrote significantly of his relationship with the dead."

"His own diary?" I asked. "You have had access to such a document?"

"Indeed, Doctor," Larkin replied. "I spend most of my days in the archives room of one of the larger universities. They have many of Silchester's originals documents including his journals.

"They are of particular interest to me because Silchester writes of the voices that he heard from beyond the grave. And, it was in his final diary entry, that he admitted that it was the voices which drove him to…murder."

"Murder?"

"Yes," Larkin said. He plucked the delicate pince-nez from his nose and massaged the bridge. "You see, the Silchester home never passed onto successive generations for, one night in the year 1666, Silchester murdered his wife and three children with a hatchet. He then turned the weapon upon himself. His last diary entry, written only moments before the bloody deed was carried out, was an admittance to what was to come and a claim that it was the voices from the grave that told him to do it."

Larkin returned the pince-nez to his nose and clasped his hands again. "It was pure coincidence that I soon found myself living in Silchester Court, you understand. I simply called around at the place after studying the original Silchester documents and discovered that there were rooms to let. In need of cheap accommodations, I moved in immediately. I wish to god that I never did. It was quite ordinary in the beginning. I spent my days at the university and my nights writing and researching. I have hopes of completing a paper on the Silchester tragedy, but I fear that I shall lose my reason before it is completed. Or worse, I fear that I may lose my life.

You see, Mr. Holmes, I have begun to hear the same voices that Elias Silchester heard over two-hundred years ago."

"When did you first hear these voices?" Holmes asked without opening his eyes.

"Three weeks ago, almost to the day," Larkin replied. "Soft, dull whispering at first. I took them to be the voices of my neighbors. But I realized quite suddenly that that is an impossibility. I live on a corner of the building so there is only one room to my right, and that is unoccupied. The whispering continued off and on yet I could not place it. And then I began to predict things. These are not mental visions, you must understand. I do not conjure up pictures of what is to come: I cannot foresee whether tomorrow shall bring with it sun or rain, but I get feelings at the oddest of times. Feelings like I knew that something was going to happen. A messenger arrived at few days ago at precisely 10.20 in the evening. He knocked on my door mistaking me for a tenant upstairs, but after I sent him on his way, I realized quite suddenly that I knew he would be there at that exact time.

"These are the sort of odd events that have been happening to me of late, Mr. Holmes, and they are occurring with great frequency. I cannot explain them other than to say that I am hearing the same voices heard by Elias Silchester…the same voices that drove him to kill."

Sherlock Holmes opened his eyes at length. "Your perturbation is not unfounded, Mr. Larkin, and I should say that I have never had a case quite like yours before."

"Then you do believe –"

"I have not taken leave of my senses, Mr. Larkin," Holmes retorted holding up a protesting hand. "In fact, I was just saying to Dr. Watson this morning that our world is built entirely upon cogent facts; not the follies and fantasies of ghosts and bogies. Nevertheless, I admit to feeling unease at your situation too. Perhaps you can answer for me a few questions. Are you well acquainted with the other tenants of Silchester Court?"

"We have a casual familiarity. Little more than that."

"And you are the most recent tenant of the building?"

"A brother and sister moved into the rooms above me only a few days after I did, but I have spoken to them little."

"Perhaps you can tell me of this messenger: the man whose presence you predicted. Had you seen him about in the building ever before?"

"Never. He was a complete stranger to me."

"And you to him? I mean, Mr. Larkin, did he seem quite surprised when you answered his call at your door?"

Larkin considered. "I should say that he was."

Holmes tapped a finger to his thin, pursed lips. "I should make a note of that in particular, Watson," he said with a glance in my direction. Then, rising from seat, Holmes began to move about the room, busying himself once more at his chemical workbench.

"Do you have nothing more for Mr. Larkin," I asked at length.

"I should imagine that there is not much more that I can do for him now," Holmes replied. "Indeed, this case – while wholly unique – is actually a simple one."

"Then what is going on at Silchester Court?" Larkin cried, jumping up from his seat. "Am I in great danger?"

"By no means," Holmes said. "I cannot confirm my suspicions until I make a visit to Silchester Court, however, I wouldn't worry any longer, Mr. Larkin. Please do feel free to keep me abreast of any curious developments. Dr. Watson will show you out."

I was taken aback by Holmes' odd behavior towards Mr. Larkin but after I assured the anxious academic that all would be right soon enough, I returned to the sitting room to confront my friend on the matter. Holmes had returned to his paraphilia, scrutinizing the contents of a beaker with unwavering keenness; as though he had not moved from that spot or fixed his eyes upon any other subject in hours.

"Holmes," I declared upon entering the room, "I must admit that you treated Mr. Larkin rudely. The poor man was frightened out of his wits and you did not give him ample time or attention. You insist that you have already solved the case and yet your refuse to enlighten he or I."

Holmes returned the beaker to the workbench. "Mr. Larkin's case illustrates the very philosophy to which I referred this morning, my dear fellow," Holmes amiably responded. "On the surface, Mr. Larkin's tale is a confounding one. Voices from the dead. Premonitions of the future. Murders from two centuries ago. And yet, even without moving from my chair, I was able to come up with at least six cogent explanations with the facts provided to us. You, my dear Watson, have allowed yourself to be led astray by the multiple veils which have shrouded you from the truth."

"And the truth is?" I asked.

Holmes raised an index. "Ah, you shall have me divulging my theories before it is time. If you recall, Watson, I never suggested that I was finished outright with the case. It is by no means solved. I cannot solve it until I have paid a visit to Mr. Larkin at Silchester Hall and from there eliminated various theories from the six possible solutions. Until then, I can do nothing."

I sighed. "And when shall you visit Mr. Larkin at Silchester Court?"

"Tomorrow? Day after tomorrow? I am presently engaged on a bit of work for Scotland Yard. The chemical solution in that beaker is of the utmost importance and I am awaiting the results from my work of this morning. It is an exceedingly complex business, Watson. Mr. Larkin's, by comparison, could not be more simple."

It could not be more simple, I thought to myself, for the rest of the day. I lounged about Baker Street in relative silence as Holmes contemplated his work as though he were a natural-born chemist. We supped early and, after losing myself in the pages of one of my preferred adventure novels all evening, I retired early; Holmes still up and about as I headed off to bed. I found sleep hard to come by, however, as the problem of Mr. Augustus Larkin still hung over me. What did Holmes know that I did not? What had he gained from Larkin's interview that had escaped my notice? Though I had not lived with Sherlock Holmes long, I knew well enough by now that he had a notorious habit of keeping things to himself; a practice which I fully begrudged.

It was early the next morning that I rose, washed, and dressed, and hurried downstairs to breakfast. The room smelt of stale tobacco smoke; Holmes had evidently been up late, but he was very much asleep as I tucked in and the morning post was delivered and placed upon the breakfast table. It was another quarter of an hour before Holmes rose and joined me. As he poured himself a cup of coffee, his long dexterous fingers sifted through the newly-arrived correspondence. His eyes fell upon a telegram of particular interest.

"From Augustus Larkin, no. 11 Silchester Court," he said, as he tore open the envelope. I watched as Holmes read the message within and he suddenly blanched. "I fear that we shall have to go to Silchester Court sooner than I anticipated."

He tossed the telegram across to me. It read:

The voices spoke again last night.

Someone is going to die. – Larkin

*

I did not know what to anticipate before we set out for Silchester Court that brisk morning, but the building which we drew up to was a hideous marvel. It was clear that at one time the tall, stone dwelling had been the seat of aristocracy. However, now it seemed as if time had decayed the whole thing. The stone façade was crumbling leaving large portions exposed to the elements. Great splotches of black mold clung to the exterior and it seemed to be slowly spreading like outstretched tendrils intent on grasping onto and swallowing what was left of the building whole. In defiance, the building almost looked as if it were trying to grow: its centuries-old design dissolving and melding into the stonework edifices that lined the street to such an extent that for a moment I knew not where Silchester Court ended the others began.

Sherlock Holmes, however, did not seem to notice any of this. Instead he bustled out of our hansom and was rapping upon the door with the head of his stick by the time that I had paid our fare and joined him. His knock was answered by a dowdy, ugly older woman who wore a tattered bonnet atop a head of frizzy, greying hair, and who dried her hands upon a dirty rag.

"What? What do you want?" she growled.

"Mr. Larkin," Holmes said. In response the woman gestured with her pointed elbow. "Number 11," she said. "Third floor."

Holmes brushed past her and stepped into the building which was no more luxurious within than it was without. We were seemingly accosted by a rickety-looking staircase which bore down on us and proved to be our only method of further ingress. We mounted the steps with trepidation listening to them *creak* and cry out with each new step we climbed until we came to the door marked eleven. Holmes knocked and the door was answered immediately by Mr. Augustus Larkin. He drew us into his room and closed the door harshly behind us.

Larkin's rooms were surprisingly spacious, but had been ravaged by the hands of time just as the rest of the building had been. The walls were cracked and shabby; the floors worn, warped, and in places showing severe signs of wood rot. There was a stove tucked away in the corner of the room and on the opposite wall was a bed. In the center of the room was a desk overflowing with Larkin's research materials and before this desk stood the man himself. We had clearly interrupted him in the middle of his toilet for he looked even more slovenly and distressed than he had looked the previous morning when he had called upon us. He was still anxiously wringing his hands and paced the room in ever-shrinking concentric circles as he spoke.

"Oh, Mr. Holmes, it was dreadful. Positively dreadful. I awoke this morning with the most intense fear. An overwhelming dread for which I simply could not account. I rose and crossed to my washstand and was in the process of splashing some tepid water on my face to calm my nerves when I felt the same strange feeling that has come over me before. And I heard the voices echoing in my head. And they said, 'Tomorrow night he will be dead and at last everything shall be complete.'"

Larkin seemed on the brink of tears. "I do not know what it means, Mr. Holmes! Who is this man who is to die? Who are these voices that foretell this man's death? I simply know no longer!"

Holmes retorted: "Calm yourself, Mr. Larkin. All shall be set to right."

Yet the academic seemed not to hear my friend. "I was doing some reading last night. I discovered that this room – my room – was Elias Silchester's own room! It was in this very room that he awoke that fateful night, wrote a few lines in his diary, and then closed it forever before he went through the house and…"

"Mr. Larkin," I interjected, "if you ask me you are giving yourself nightmares reading this ghoulish material at night. I myself would never read a penny dreadful before going to bed else I shouldn't sleep a wink."

"But I have an iron constitution, Dr. Watson," Larkin replied. "I have never suffered from nightmares before. And certainly, never like this."

Holmes, meanwhile, was pacing the room. "You are indeed the last room on this floor," he said. "And you say that the room next door is vacant?"

"Yes," Larkin replied. "I tell you, Mr. Holmes, that I have considered more than once moving rooms. This one is surely cursed. Perhaps I could escape from all these terrible voices and awful premonitions if I laid my head somewhere else."

Holmes rocked back and forth on his feet, gently undulating from heel to toe. "Please do not purchase the room next to this one, Mr. Larkin."

"Why? Why should I not try to save myself from all of this?"

"Because, Mr. Larkin," Holmes replied. "I should like to buy it."

"You!" I cried. "Holmes, why on earth should you wish to buy a room here?"

"Baker Street is all well and good to rest my head at nights, Watson, and to entertain clients, but in my line, I do find myself requiring more than one base of operations in the city. A room here in Silchester Court would do admirably.

"And what is more," Holmes said, "if I purchase a room here in Silchester Court, then I can lend it to you for no charge at all this evening, Mr. Larkin."

"Then you will let me escape this place?"

"Yes," answered Holmes, "provided you allow Dr. Watson and I the use of it this evening."

"You can have it!" Larkin cried. "I want nothing to do with it at all."

Holmes smiled a wry grin. "And you can do me another favor, Mr. Larkin. I am exceedingly interested in reading the diary of Elias Silchester. Would you take me to the archive room this afternoon so I read up on it myself?"

The academic replied in the affirmative and asked for a few moments to prepare himself. We stepped out into the hall.

"You really don't want a room here do you, Holmes?" I asked.

"Nonsense, Watson," my friend replied. "I have no need for lodgings in Silchester Court. But I do want the use of Mr. Larkin's room this evening – that shall, I think, prove quite instructive – and I figured I should spare the poor man any further anguish. Now, that we have a few minutes to ourselves, I should like to continue my investigation on the floor above."

On the next floor, Holmes paced back and forth about the hall for a few moments. Then, eyeing one of the doors in particular, he approached and knocked politely. His call was answered by a dark-haired young woman. She was simply dressed and her response to Holmes' intrusion into her life was answered with forthrightness which bordered on brusqueness.

"May I help you?" she asked.

"Yes, madam," Holmes replied. "I'm a prospective tenant in this building and I was hoping that my solicitor and I –" Holmes gestured wide to me behind him "– could have a look about your flat? You know, to see if it's dissimilar to the room I've got my eye on below. You hear such tales, you know, madam, of unscrupulous landlords who will entice you with a fine, fine dwelling, only for your actual residence to be something far, far less decorous."

"I am afraid sir," the woman replied, "that I am quite occupied at the moment and cannot spare you any of your time."

She attempted to close the door on my friend but he stuck his foot into the jamb. "But, madam," he said, "surely you have sympathy for a concerned buyer in your heart. I merely wish to have a look 'round. I shan't be but a moment."

"Sorry, sir," she retorted and closed the door in Holmes' face. He spun around, an odd smile upon his face. Then, silencing me with a look, he gestured that we return to meet with Mr. Larkin.

"What could you have possibly gained from that?" I inquired as Holmes and I retraced our steps down the stairs.

"I learned precisely what I wanted to know, my dear Watson," Holmes answered. "Ah, and here is Mr. Larkin too. Our timing could not have been better. I think, Watson, that I shall be dull company for much of the day. Let us meet at

Baker Street for a late luncheon where I shall hopefully bear the fruits of today's labor."

The three of us quit the building, only to run into the landlady on the ground floor, foolheartedly scrubbing at a spot of mold on the wall which was surely as immoveable as a mountain. Holmes stopped the woman in her task and presented himself as a prospective tenant. Claiming to have a full months' rent on his person, he said he was most interested in the vacant room next to Mr. Larkin's. He dropped a bag of coins into the woman's palm and she stared into it as if hypnotized.

"Perhaps," Holmes said, "you can be of aide to my friends and I in one other matter. You see, madam, I am something of an amateur photographer and I would be most interested in setting up a dark room in this building. I trust there is a cellar?"

"Aye, there is," the woman replied. "No one goes down there. On account of the stories, I suppose."

"Stories?" I asked. "What kind of stories?"

The woman shrugged her shoulders. "Ghost stories, I'd expect."

We did as Holmes suggested and he returned elated early that evening just as the sun was sinking beneath the horizon throwing long shadows about our rooms and bathing us both in shades of muted orange and red. It was the perfect setting for our somber meal and, after we finished, Holmes pushed his chair back and stretched himself out before he reached for his pipe.

"The diary of Elias Silchester could not have been more fascinating," he began. "It was truly a remarkable study, especially to a student of crime like me. I confess that before yesterday, I hadn't heard the name Silchester nor had I known of the remarkable tragedy which befell him and his family."

"Remarkable indeed," I said. "The senseless, brutal murder of four people – an entire household. It curdles the blood."

"There I am afraid that you are incorrect," Holmes replied, pulling on his pipe. "I do not deny that the affair does curdle the blood, but the murder of four innocent people did not constitute the eradication of an entire household. There was a fifth member of Silchester Court there that evening whose name, it seems, is lost to the pages of history entirely. That of Silchester's cousin, a name called Lewis Grayale. His presence in our narrative sheds new light upon the entire business and all but confirms many of the suspicions that I had regarding this case."

"I confess that I am entirely lost."

From his breast pocket, Holmes withdrew a sheet of paper. "That," he said, "is a transcription of the last diary entry of Elias Silchester before the murder of his family and his suicide. It is copied word for word from his journal which Mr. Larkin and I studied all of the day. Read it and tell me if anything strikes you as significant."

I took up the sheet and read what Holmes had copied:

January 9:

I fear that I cannot abide the voices any longer. They have become louder and more persistent of late. No longer are they simply the hushed whispers of the world beyond; these are the full-throated shouts of malignant beings and they have but one instruction for me: to kill. To kill. To kill. They say that I shall never be free if I do not kill and I fear that they are right. If I wish to silence these blasted demons and return them to whatever pit from whence they have crawled, then I must do as they wish.

I do not do what I do out of malice or out of lust (as I am sure my enemies shall suggest in the days to come). I simply do what I must do to save myself and save my soul. Surely once I have left this earth, I can find peace; at last separated from the voices that are damned to whisper in my ears and drive me to do what I do. Peace. That is all that a man could want. Peace. This is my only way to get it.

The hatchet blade is sharp and shined. It shall serve its purpose well –

It was bone-chilling stuff and I handed the sheet back to Holmes with a tremor agitating my fingers.

"Do you not find it suggestive?"

"I find it repulsive," I said. "It is undoubtedly a full confession of guilt."

"Tut, tut, Watson," Sherlock Holmes said. "Have I not taught you that there is nothing more deceptive than an obvious fact? Does this diary entry reveal to you nothing more than a desperate man's last moments on earth?"

I reconsidered what I had just read. "The voices," I said at length. "Silchester says that they got louder in the end."

Holmes struck the tabletop with an open palm. "Excellent, Watson. We shall make you a first-rate detective yet. You have picked up on the mot pertinent piece of information in the entire diary."

"Are you saying that someone – perhaps this Grayale man – was the one speaking to Silchester? That he lured Silchester in murdering his entire family?"

"That is precisely what I am suggesting and I believe that much the same is happening to our unfortunate Mr. Larkin."

"How? Both Silchester and Larkin were alone in their rooms? Their rooms are on the corner of the building. No one could possibly speak to them from the third-story window without floating in the air like some phantasm. And I know you well enough, Holmes, to know you reject that possibility outright. Granted, this Grayale character may have been speaking to Silchester through the wall on the opposite side of the room, but we know that to be impossible in Larkin's case as the room is unoccupied. Someone may have stolen in there at nights, but what with the way the whole building creaks it would be near impossible for someone to stealthily move about without Larkin knowing. And what is more, I cannot see any reason to drive a poor, down-on-his-luck academic mad."

"You fail to grasp the magnitude of this case," Holmes replied. "In doing so, you have managed to isolate nearly every point of importance and yet failed to interpret them as you should. What you have failed to grasp, Watson, is that Mr. Augustus Larkin is but a tangential element in this case. He is not and never was the point of focus."

"I am afraid that I do not understand."

Holmes stood and began to make a circuit about the room as was his habit when in the depths of oration.

"Over two-hundred years ago," he began, "Mr. Lewis Grayale conjured up a devious method of murder. He would masquerade as the spirit voices that he knew his cousin, Elias, to listen to and use them to influence Elias Silchester into murdering his entire family and himself. Then, no doubt with no family left to claim the substantial estate that would remain following Silchester's death, Grayale could claim it and abscond with it. No wonder then that Silchester Court fell into such ruin and disrepair with no one occupying the seat who would maintain it.

"Now, two centuries on, history is repeating itself but merely by happenstance. Mr. Larkin has quite unwittingly stumbled into the midst of a plot which is no doubt just as devious as the one perpetrated by Lewis Grayale in the seventeenth century."

"But what is going on?" I cried. "Who is perpetrating this scheme and what exactly do they wish to accomplish?"

Holmes plucked a photograph from his voluminous record collection. "Did you by chance recognize the face of the young woman who answered the door today at Silchester Court?"

"I must admit that I did not. Should I?"

"If you paid a little less attention to cricket scores and more time to the society pages of *The Times*, then perhaps you might have."

Holmes plucked up a newssheet and dropped it on the table alongside the picture. Staring up at me was a photograph of three persons, two men and a woman. Seated in the middle of the photo was a distinguished-looking, white-bearded man. On either side of him, standing over him, were two young people: the woman in the photo undoubtedly the same that we had seen earlier in the day. My eyes moved to the newspaper.

Financial Tycoon at Death's Door?

I stared at the bold headline, then my eyes fell upon the newsprint written beneath:

Reports remain unsubstantiated but it is believed that financial tycoon G.J. Petty, the business magnet formerly of Kanas, USA, is in poor health. His recent absences from share-holder's meetings have worried many close to the Petty family though his son, Arthur, insists that there is nothing with which to be concerned. Though he admits that his father has been battling frequent bouts of fatigue, he insists that the patriarch of the Petty family is hale and healthy.

Arthur Petty, our readers may well recall, recently married Catherine O'Martin, formerly of Baltimore, Maryland, and daughter of the noted American senator Thaddeus Martin. The wedding was the talk of English aristocracy last May when the couple was married at Petty's country estate in Kent.

"Do you not smell deviltry, Watson," Sherlock Holmes asked.

"Are you suggesting that this O'Martin woman, Petty's daughter-in-law, is conspiring to murder him?"

Holmes returned to his chair. "It is the perfect scheme, Watson: Catherine O'Martin takes up residence at Silchester Court, a crumbling tenement building in Soho where it is certain that she shall go unrecognized. The locale is an odd one, but I do believe that it was not chosen at random. Though records were hard to come by, I would wager a great deal that Lewis Grayale, after fleeing England, escaped to the new world and established himself in parts unknown. I believe it is no great leap to suggest that the Petty family are descendants of Lewis Grayale; distant relations of the Silchester family and therefore still had legal claim over Silchester Court in London. From there, she establishes a base of operations where she may conduct her illicit business; notably the importation of deadly poisons with which she may slowly poison her father-in-law, masking his wasting away as another battle of fatigue. I have no doubt that the messenger who arrived in the night and who mistook Larkin's room for hers is her co-conspirator.

"But this business goes deeper still. You recall exactly who is living above Larkin's room, do you not, Watson?"

"He said a brother and a sister." The truth dawned on me at once. "You do not mean to suggest that Petty's son is involved too! That they are masquerading as a brother and sister and are conspiring together to murder Petty?"

"The man sits upon a fortune which would drive you or I to distraction," Holmes intoned. "Surely it a sum that would drive any man or woman to commit desperate acts. Tonight, we must catch them in the act and bring their scheme to an end. We do not have much time. You recall what Larkin heard the voices say: 'Tomorrow night he will be dead.'"

Suddenly Holmes sprang into action. He had jumped up from his seat and was reaching for his hat and coat. "Do be so good as to drop a bulls-eye lantern into your pocket, Watson. We shall be in need of it tonight."

As we readied ourselves, I turned to my friend and asked: "I must know: what did you hope to see in Catherine O'Martin's room this afternoon?"

"I saw exactly what I wanted to see," Holmes replied. "I wanted to see if her room was the same as Larkin's. It was not. Larkin has a stove."

*

It was just past 8.00 but the city was already wrapped in the fog of night when we returned to Silchester Court. By dark, the dwelling took on an even more menacing aspect; a great, dark mass which looked down upon us as we approached. Holmes rapped upon the door and was greeted by the same woman who had answered his call earlier in the day.

Holmes tipped his hat to the woman who let her well-paying newest tenant past without a word and started up the creaky steps, gesturing for me to follow. Once we had reached the top, he knocked upon Mr. Larkin's door. The academic answered it in a frenzy.

"Calm yourself, Mr. Larkin," Holmes hissed. "Your ordeal is nearly over. I have gained you access to room number 10. If you do not mind roughing it for a few hours, I imagine that I can return you to the safety of your own bed in a few hours' time."

"Safety? Safety? I cannot think of a more dangerous place in the whole world than that god-forsaken room," Larkin said.

"I think that I shall be able to disprove that, sir," Holmes said. Then, sending the man on his way, Holmes stepped inside the room and closed the door after me.

"I do not think that we shall need to wait long," Sherlock Holmes said as he took a seat. "Make yourself as comfortable as possible, Watson, but keep your wits about you. I suspect that soon you will witness something which, on the face of it, cannot be reconciled with the settled order of nature."

So, we waited. From time to time I consulted my watch as I watched the minutes crawl by. It was gone 10.30 when I first thought I heard something. I looked to Holmes and saw his ears perk up as though he were a vigilant watchdog. He stood from his seat and gestured for me to follow him across the room. I approached apprehensively stopping just before the low stove that was wedged into the corner of the room. It struck me suddenly that the sounds I heard were emanating from the stove itself. They sounded garbled and distant, inhuman almost, as though the natural intonations of the human voice had been distorted by the shrill sound of a hand playing the glasses. However, as I concentrated, I could make out the words being spoken:

"He arrives tonight. 11.15. It will be the last shipment. Then, I will return home and administer the final dose. We return by the servant stairs as if nothing has happened."

In that instant, everything seemed to fall into place. I felt Holmes' iron grip upon my forearm.

"Now, Watson," he said. "Grab the bulls-eye and follow me."

I scooped up the lantern from where I had placed it upon Larkin's desk and followed Holmes into the dark passageway. We were met with impenetrable, inky blackness, and I groped with the flaps upon the light as we made our way blindly towards the staircase. Holmes took each one with great care as to not emit any sound as we descended and once we had arrived on the ground floor, he hastened his steps towards the rear of the building; no doubt in search of the entranceway to the cellar. We found the door in due course and wrenching it open, we descended; I rushing after my friend. I heard the sound of commotion below and when I reached the landing at the bottom, I found Holmes poised before both the man I knew to be Arthur Petty and the woman that was his wife, with his cane at the ready in defense.

Two hours later, Holmes and I were back within the familiar environs of Baker Street. I was nursing a glass of brandy before the fire, while Holmes packed his pipe with his strong shag tobacco. Our attention was focused on our guest,

Mr. Augustus Larkin, who, for the first time since we had made his acquaintance, did not look quite so perturbed.

"From the beginning I asserted that this case was a simple one," Holmes began, striking a match and easing back in his chair. "Rejecting an otherworldly explanation for the voices that you heard, Mr. Larkin, and from the position of your room in the building, I knew that they must have originated from somewhere in Silchester Court. It became, then, a matter of divining where they came from in the building and what they meant. I combated numerous theories, but the pieces of the puzzle began to fall into place when I visited Silchester Court for myself this morning.

"I noted the singular fact that you were staying in what was at one time Elias Silchester's own room. Your room, then, would undoubtedly be different from nearly every other chamber in the building, belonging as it did to the master of the house. I was proven right in this regard when I saw that you had what appeared to be a stove in your room. However, the room above yours, belonging to Mr. Arthur Petty and his wife, did not. Coupling this fact with the knowledge that Silchester Court was at one time a house, I came to the conclusion that what appeared to be a stove in your room, Mr.

Larkin, was in fact a small fireplace. It therefore required a heat source from elsewhere which suggested that there was some means of transporting the heat from one part of the building to the other: a system of heating pipes with their origin in the basement.

"In this way, I developed a theory which explained how Elias Silchester's cousin, Lewis Grayale, was able to convince his cousin that the spirits' voices were speaking to him, and how Mr. Larkin was hearing voices of his own. Grayale, hiding in the cellar, would merely have to speak into the fireplace in the cellar and his voice would carry up through the ducts and into Silchester's room. Grayale plotted the murder of Silchester's family and, with the residue of the estate to claim, he disappeared entirely.

"Curiously, Mr. Larkin's voices were also tied to murder, but these voices were not intentional. Arthur Petty and his wife, fearful that they may be overheard by someone in their own room, took to conferring in the cellar by night. Unbeknownst to them, their voices too traveled up through the pipes and into Mr. Larkin's room. As he slept, he became an unwilling eavesdropping on their schemes and, in the morning, would awake with memories and knowledge he did not know he had."

Holmes laid aside his pipe. "As usual," he said, "the truth proves to be simplicity itself. And with a little rational cognition not only have we uncovered the truth of your case, Mr. Larkin, but brought to a close a case which has remained open for over two-centuries. And now that we have brought this matter to a resolution, Mr. Larkin, I have but one more suggestion for you."

"What is that, Mr. Holmes?"

"Get yourself some well-deserved sleep."

The Adventure of the Deadly Inheritance

I shall forever regard the fifth of November in the year '87 to be one of the most remarkable in all my years with that equally remarkable man, Mr. Sherlock Holmes. It was during this period that Holmes and I were sharing rooms as bachelors in Baker Street, yet, in the days leading up to that extraordinary case, I had seen little of my companion. His habit of disappearing for hours – indeed, on occasion days at a time – I had become used to, but now, his intermittent appearances in our sitting room were marked by a singular nervous energy. He would barely greet me when I entered the room; instead, drumming his anxious fingers on the arm of his chair while he chomped on his pipe and stared, brow furrowed, into the flames dancing in the fireplace. Then, sudden animation would touch his limbs, and he'd be up and about the room, digging into the depths of his index, before gathering up hat and coat, and disappearing out into the night with the speed and ferocity of a hurricane.

I knew better then to question Holmes knowing full well that he would explain his actions when he was ready.

That time came on that fateful November evening. A thick grey fog had descended over London, hushing the metropolis like a mother would her babe. In this instance however, the quiet had taken on an eerie aspect with the streets devoid of life, and the flickering orange glow of the gas lamps rendered tiny points of light in the unforgiving shroud. I had returned to our rooms after conducting some business early in the day to find Holmes in his usual chair by the fire. He was wrapped in his preferred dressing gown, his chin to his breast, the stem of his long Cherrywood pipe protruding from his thin, cruel lips. I had settled in with a glass of restorative brandy and was reaching for the latest edition of *The Times* when my friend's sudden exclamation drew my attention.

"The press has been uncharacteristically taciturn in their reporting," he said. I confessed that I had not seen the paper yet that day and, unfolding himself from his seat, Holmes indicated a headline with the stem of his pipe. My eyes went to the bold black print:

Solicitor Murdered, Scotland Yard Baffled

There followed a brief paragraph which I scanned quickly only to find that Holmes' words rang true. Powerful attorney, Adrian Crawley, had been found murdered in his home on Wednesday, the second of that month. He had been bludgeoned to death and, beyond the ferocity with which the crime had been committed, the principle feature of the case was that Crawley's body was discovered in his study, the door to which had been locked from within. I set the paper aside to see my friend's eyes dancing with excitement.

"It is a pretty little problem," he said. He leaned back in his seat, effecting the air of a storyteller. "Though I am afraid that, despite my best efforts, there has been little progress in the investigation. It is Gregson's case."

"Which means," I interjected, "that he's liable to go and arrest the wrong person."

My jest brought a smile to Holmes' face. "Gregson called here on Wednesday morning just after the body was found. On the cab ride to Crawley's house, I had to convince the Inspector not to arrest the entirety of Crawley's household staff for complicity in their employer's murder." Holmes pulled on his pipe contemplatively. "There has been little data of consequence," he said. "As the press reports, Crawley's study was locked from the inside. His domestic staff all have solid alibis for the time of the murder. The sheer *impossibility* of it all is what has intrigued me from the beginning."

"Are there no suspects?"

Holmes waved his hand flippantly. "There are too many," he replied. "Crawley was employed by some of London's most powerful names. My main course of action these past few days has been to follow up with as many of them as possible. It has been no mean feat, I can assure you. My researches have taken me from the hallowed corridors of Whitehall to the darkest streets of Limehouse."

"Limehouse?"

"Yes, Doctor. Though I am sure that Crawley would have wished for his reputation to remain lily-white, there numbered among his clients several who – to put it delicately – run with an *unsavory sort*. Just yesterday evening, I called upon one of these gentlemen in my own person and received this for my pains."

He extended his hand and I noticed for the first time the harsh red gash that ran across his knuckles. I moved to fetch my medical bag, but Holmes stopped me with a mild protestation.

"You needn't worry yourself, Doctor. I helped myself to some of the things from your Gladstone bag. It is but a scratch, I assure you. The gentleman who inflicted this wound with his straight razor was quite taken off his guard when I managed to slip a revolver from my pocket and press it to his temple. The wound may have smarted on the cab ride home, hut it was worth the intelligence gathered in the end."

"And what, may I ask, did you learn from this unsavory character?"

"Nothing."

"Nothing?"

The wry smile touched Holmes' lips again. "Not even Crawley's most unscrupulous clients had cause to see the man dead. Each new dead-end in this investigation complicates the case further, but succeeds in intriguing me all the more."

I asked Holmes what he intended to do next. To my surprise, he shrugged his shoulders. "I shall wait," he said with an uncharacteristic air of nonchalance. "The murder of Adrian Crawley may seem, on the surface, to be a perfect crime, but the perpetrator can only keep up his façade for so long. While Gregson continues to wear out his boot leather in pursuit of the truth, I shall sit and wait and let the answer come to me."

I acquiesced to my friend's curious decision and, after pouring two brandies for the both of us, I stepped to the window to cast a glance out into the night. It was impossible to perceive anything beyond the pane of glass. For a moment, I felt bricked in by the wall of fog; the uncomfortable sensation broken a moment later by the ring of the bell below. I looked to Holmes and asked if he expected a caller to which he replied in the negative. A moment later, Mrs. Hudson appeared in the doorway presenting a card.

"Edmund Ainsford," Holmes said reading from the card. "The name does perhaps strike the ear, but I cannot be certain. Do you know him, Watson?"

I confessed that I did not and Holmes sent the landlady away with instructions to show the man up at once. The man who entered the sitting room a moment later was one of the most curious specimens who had ever crossed our threshold. He was a small man, yet possessed of broad shoulders, and a curious egg-shaped head which he had cocked to one side. He was no more than thirty, and his youthful, ruddy features only doubled the peculiarity of his appearance. As he entered, he turned his gaze from Holmes then to me before inquiring which of us was the man he sought.

"I am Sherlock Holmes," my friend said with a courtly air, "and this is my friend and colleague, Dr. Watson. Pray take a seat, Mr. Ainsford."

The little man obliged, settling himself into the basket chair and holding his hands to the fire. "I am ever so pleased to find you in, sir," he said, and for the first time I detected a palpable anxiety about his person. He spoke in a nasally tone, marked with a twinge of uncompromised fear. "I come to you in a state of great desperation."

"It is not an unusual state for my clients," Holmes replied. "Tell me Mr. Ainsford, you wouldn't happen to be related to Sir Ian Ainsford?"

"He was my uncle," the man replied. "You are, no doubt, familiar with his meat pies?"

"I cannot say that I am," Holmes said, "but I have, on occasion, known Dr. Watson to enjoy such a treat." I flushed despite myself. "Your uncle is, I take it, one of the premier meat manufacturers in this country, Mr. Ainsford."

"That he is," Edmund Ainsford replied. "Yet the matter that brings me to you is – thankfully – not linked up with his business." He drew in a deep breath. "You must find my brother, Mr. Holmes."

"Your brother? He has gone missing?"

"Disappeared. Without trace."

"When was this, Mr. Ainsford?"

"Just this evening. I do hope that the trail has not yet gone cold."

"Perhaps," Holmes said, "you ought to start at the beginning. Omit nothing at all, Mr. Ainsford."

Holmes settled back in his chair, closing his eyes as if in a state of deep satisfaction as our client began to speak.

"What you must first understand, above all else, gentleman, is the *ritual*. You see, my uncle was the eldest son and therefore inherited the burgeoning business. My own father, the younger son, was left with little in my grandfather's will and elected to pass on something else to his own kin. He created the ritual; a rite of passage for all Ainsford sons when they came of age. My father died several years ago and his last request was that my brother perform the ritual when the time came. Well, yesterday was my brother's twenty-fifth birthday and, earlier this evening, we together went about performing the ritual."

"What does this ritual entail?" I asked.

"I do not know the specifics," our client replied. "The instructions were outlined in a document that my father drew up before his death. This document was then entrusted to our family solicitor and only turned over to my brother, Cedric, early this week. He, in turn, looked over the document and then began to set things in motion with little assistance from me. However, early this evening, he asked that I accompany him. I could not refuse the request from my own brother and, I must add, that curiosity drove me to wanting to uncover the truth behind as much of this family secret as possible.

"Per Cedric's instructions, we acquired a cab, my brother calling out an address in Wapping. As we took off into the night, I questioned him and he told me that the document left by our father instructed that he call upon that address. He also told me that he must go to a singular room within the building and, therein, he would find his 'inheritance.'"

"His inheritance?" Holmes spoke for the first time, his eyes still tightly closed in deep contemplation.

"Yes. Apparently the ritual was to lead to my brother's own inheritance, quite separate from that of the family business."

"Was your father a wealthy man?" I asked.

"He was an adventurer," Ainsford replied. "While my uncle stayed in England and built up the family empire, my father was traveling the world. From what I gather – he was always distant from Cedric and I, you understand – he spent some considerable time in China and Australia. There were always rumors that he had struck gold in Australia but, then again, that was simply a story."

"Pray continue, Mr. Ainsford."

Our client wrung his hands anxiously. "Our cab deposited us in a dilapidated corner of Wapping, on a most inauspicious street. A series of crumbling houses loomed down at us; their darkened windows, in the harsh fog, looking more like judgmental eyes. I confess to feeling a thrill of true terror as the carriage eased to a stop. Even our cabbie seemed most insistent on leaving the neighborhood. Cedric was undaunted.

"'If all goes well,' he promised our driver, 'then I shall pay for our fare ten-fold!'

"I grabbed at his arm in the dark of the cab and impressed upon my brother that the promise was a dangerous one, especially in our present surroundings. The fog had grown so thick at this point that, peering out of the window into the night, I could barely divine the outlines of the rotting old piles on the street opposite, and that particular stretch of road seemed to vanish into infinity. What unknown horrors there were that lay hidden out there unseen, I knew not. Cedric was undaunted. From his waistcoat pocket, he produced a key and pressed it into my palm.

"'This key,' he said with an air of genuine triumph, 'is my destiny.'

"Then he jumped down out of the carriage and disappeared into the fog. I strained to hear his progress and I knew that he had successfully made it to the opposite side of the street by the sound of his footfalls echoing in that quiet side street. Then, I swear to hearing a door being opened, then shut. That is the last that I saw of my brother on this earth."

I confess that I felt the same thrill of horror that Mr. Ainsford must have felt as he told us his tale. The low light of the gas lamps, and the shadows of the flickering fire dancing a macabre ballet on the walls, with the oppressive veil of fog outside gave me pause. I looked to Holmes who sat unmoving; the smoke rising from his pipe and circling his pointed features the tell-tale sign that he breathed still. This moment of quiet – which seemingly passed for much longer – was broken by one of my companion's characteristic sudden exclamations:

"What did you do next?"

"I waited," came our client's response. "When I had heard the door closed, I sat poised in the carriage anticipating his eventual return. When nearly ten minutes had passed, and I heard nothing from Cedric, I alighted from the cab and began to cross the street with the utmost trepidation. I had only gone a few feet when I heard the cabbie crack his whip behind me, and the cab raced off into the fog. I considered giving chase, but I feared that I should become gravely lost in the fog. Besides, the overwhelming desire to make sure that no ill had come to my brother propelled me forward.

"I came upon the same door through which Cedric had managed his ingress and, much to my surprise, I found it still unlocked. I stepped into the building and closed the door behind me. Inside, I found a set of candles and a box of matches laid out. I picked one up, lit the candle, and discovered that I was in the front room of what, at one time, must have been an old rooming house. There was a front sitting room seemingly untouched in ages, for a thick layer of dust now coated the floor and touched nearly every other surface, including a few pieces of broken-down furniture. Immediately in front of me was a narrow staircase leading up into the house and there was also a long corridor that must have gone out to the rear of the building. This too was covered in a layer of unbroken dust. The only footprints I could divine in the dim light of my candle were a single set that ascended the stairs. Mustering all the courage I could, I called out to my brother and, when no response came, I mounted the steps and climbed to the first floor.

"The house was quiet as death; the nearly imperceptible hissing and popping of my candle flame proving to be the only sound I could discern. When I reached the top of the stairs, I continued to follow Cedric's footprints. They lead to a door in the rear of the house. I tried the door and found it locked from within."

Holmes opened his eyes slowly and leaned forward in his chair. "The key? Was it still in the lock?"

"I did kneel down to examine the lock and it did look as if that was the case."

"Did you force down the door?"

"I did. I had no choice. I gravely suspected that some harm had come to my brother and I greatly feared what it was that I would find on the other side of that door. I am not a strong man, Mr. Holmes, but I did muster up the energy to throw my whole weight against the door. It was old, rotted wood, and I managed to break the door from it hinges in one go. Never in my wildest dreams could I have suspected what it was that I would find in that room.

"The room was square. Quite small. Only a few feet by few feet. I must imagine that the chamber must have been a child's room at some point judging by its size and, indeed, the once colorful wallpaper that, in places, still clung in decaying patches to the wall. In the center of the room was a low table. There on the tabletop was a candle placed directly into an old holder. The candle must have belonged to my brother for the wax had not yet begun to drip. It had only just been lighted a few minutes earlier. Yet, of my brother, there was no sign. He had entered that room and then disappeared without a trace."

The same silence fell over our room, filled anew with the air of disquiet and palpable unease that had settled over the room from the moment Edmund Aisnford had stepped through our threshold. Sherlock Holmes, wearing the most unusual mask of gratification, sat back in his chair and laid his pipe aside.

"Your case, Mr. Ainsford," he began, "is singular. The details are quite unlike anything that has hitherto been presented to me."

A look of intense consternation crossed Ainsford's round face. "You cannot help me?"

"On the contrary, Mr. Ainsford," Holmes replied, "I shall do everything I can to bring this matter to as satisfying a conclusion as possible."

"Oh, thank you, Mr. Holmes.

"Though I intend to bring this matter to a conclusion this night, all my resources are directed toward another case at present. I cannot afford to leave Baker Street when I expect a resolution at any moment."

"Then what can you do?"

"I shall assign to you my very best man," Holmes said. His gaze turned in my direction. "Dr. Watson shall accompany you back to that house in Wapping. You do think that you could return there if you had to?"

"Yes. I shall forever remember that address that Cedric gave to the cabbie."

Holmes stood and rubbed his hands together with zeal. "Excellent! I shall conduct what research I can from here, but you may be assured that my dear Watson's vivacity in matters of this sort is equal to my own."

Edmund Ainsford stood and wrung the detective warmly by the hand. "I cannot thank you enough."

Holmes consulted his watch. "The hour grows late, my good sir, so you had best procure a cab for you and the Doctor. I fear that hailing one may be somewhat difficult in this weather, however –"

Holmes dug into his pocket, producing a coin which he pressed into our client's palm.

"– Flash this in the eye of even the most recalcitrant of cabbies, and I suspect that you shan't have too much trouble."

With a gleeful glint in his once-terrified eyes, Edmund Ainsford disappeared out of the sitting room. As soon as the door closed behind him, a sudden change came over Holmes. There came into his eye the steely determination of the big game hunter who lies in wait for the tiger to cross his path. So sudden, and so violent was the transformation that I was taken aback.

"This is a grisly business, Watson," he said.

"You think there is some danger in all this?" I asked.

"Oh, that much is obvious," came his dark reply. "I think you would find it prudent to slip your revolver into your pocket and have all your wits about you."

I moved to my desk, slipping the cold steel of the firearm into my pocket. As I shrugged on my coat, I cast another look toward my friend who stood, looking out of the window and into the foggy night.

"Holmes," I asked. "What does this all mean?"

"It means murder, Watson. Do be careful tonight my friend."

Ensconced in the belly of a hansom cab beside Ainsford, I thought back to the dark expression Holmes wore as he bade me farewell. His warning of danger chilled my blood and I wondered what evil it was that we would face when we came to the end of our journey. As our cab trundled through the night, we sliced through the dense fog, but we were merely an island in a sea of nothingness. As far as the eye could see, there extended the great blanket of grey which wreathed the buildings and streetlamps. Our carriage, winding through one neighborhood, and then another, would come upon groves of distant light emanating from behind the windows of the houses we passed, but these fleeting glimpses of civilization were all I had to cling to. Were it not for the watch in my waistcoat, I suspect that I should have been lost in both space and time, as though I were adrift on an endless sea.

What only increased the disquiet of that night was the haunting songs that I heard drifting from some point in the distance. As I peered through the window of the carriage, I detected the outline of a great bonfire; a misshapen mound of wood set alight. The merest outline of this curious spectacle would be seen from our cab, and so caught up was in our present business that I very nearly forgot that it was Guy Fawkes' Night; the pyre the product of the local children's eerie taste for blood and vengeance against the centuries-old traitor. In the night, their gruesome rhymes, disconnected to their dancing forms around the bonfire, sounded like the incantations a witch might have spouted over her cauldron:

Guy, Guy, Guy
Poke him in the eye
Put him on the bonfire
And there let him die

At length, our cab came to a stop and Ainsford and I stepped out of the carriage onto the cobblestone pavement. The stretch of road on which we stood was just as the man had described: a lonely side-street seemingly cut off from the rest of the city. Even here, the children's song that had earlier eerily filled the night air was hushed and distant. We looked up at a row of crumbling tenements, all derelict and unoccupied. The only sound to be heard in that place of utter desolation was the rhythmic lapping of the Thames not far afield. Through the night, I thought I heard the low hum of a barge's horn, and, in turning to place the sound, I suddenly found myself accosted by a dark shape that leapt out of the night.

I let out a cry and fought back, striking out with a hand. I managed to untangle myself from whatever it was that had grabbed a hold of me. Ainsford and I looked at the thing; at first little more than a black mass in the dark, but I soon discovered it to be a man. He was a short, scruffy-looking creature, dressed in tattered clothes, and several-days growth of hair on his pointed features. His sudden manifestation and appearance so unnerved me that I sputtered in reprimanding him.

"The blackguard was no doubt after my purse," I declared.

From beneath the brim of a wide black hat, the man emitted a wheezy chuckle. "Just after a bit of food, guv," he said. "This part of the world is no place for a toff like you."

"We haven't any money," Ainsford said. "And you had best be running along before we call for the police."

The man only laughed in response. "The police?! You think they care for what's going on down here?!" He suddenly held out his hands like an orphan pleading for food in the workhouse. "Please, guv," he implored, "just a bob or two. You *must* have that!"

I quickly reached into my pocket and produced a coin, tossing it to the ground. The man immediately dived after it; his dirt-stained hands clambering in the road for his prize. I watched him pick it up with his blackened fingernails and he hid his loot away into the folds of his dark clothes.

"Thank you very much guv," he said. "Thank you very much."

And then, as quickly as this apparition had appeared, he had gone, scuttling off into the night.

"What a horrible place," Ainsford breathed. "There seem to be some very dangerous people about in this place. You don't think…Cedric, I mean…"

"Mr. Holmes did not tell me what to think," I lied, remembering all too well that word that now hung about my neck like the albatross: *murder*. "But, he did insist that I bring this." I tapped the revolver in my breast pocket reassuringly.

"Well thank god for that," Ainsford said, relief flooding his words. "Perhaps you had best see for yourself what it was that I found this night."

I gestured for Ainsford to lead us both and we started across the street toward the dark outline of the house. As we approached, I had the sudden sense that the place was looking down on us; its shape taking form out of the wall of fog. Ainsford has not been wrong when he said that the darkened windows resembled inscrutable eyes, and approaching the front door suddenly felt as if we were walking into the belly of the beast. I cast a nervous glance over my shoulder and, through the night, I could have sworn that I divined the shape of the horrible creature that had accosted Ainsford and me still loitering in the dark, attempting to conceal himself in the doorway of a building beyond. I thought of saying something, but I knew how fearful Ainsford was and did not wish to frighten him into perhaps abandoning our mission.

From his pocket, Ainsford produced a key and inserted it into the lock of the front door. It swung open and we stepped into the front room. When he closed the door behind us, I was filled with a sudden twinge of relief, until my eyes fell upon the empty room that greeted us. It was just as he had described it: a disused front room to a boarding house, the place having long-since fallen into disrepair. There was only one feature of the room that did not correspond with Ainsford's description and I pointed it out to him as soon as my eyes fell upon it:

"There's another set of footprints."

Indeed, where Ainsford had said there had been only one set left by his brother, there now appeared two more. One, I took to be our client's, but the other was totally unaccounted for. This set crisscrossed the front room several times, each time leading to the far wall. As I stepped further into the room, careful not to disrupt the prints that remained, I took note of a large rectangular spot on the floor where the dust had been clearly disturbed.

"What could that be?"

Ainsford approached. "I should think the impression of a case."

The gruesome image of some unknown person – perhaps even the stranger in the room – pressing the body of Cedric Ainsford into a large trunk sprang into my mind. I shook my head to expunge the grim notion, scolding myself as Holmes might have for allowing me to theorize before we were in possession of all the facts. I stood to my full height and instructed our man to take me to the room at the top of the stairs. Ainsford nodded his head and we started up the narrow staircase; each step emitting a loud *squeak* as we did. The sound echoed through the cavernous dwelling, calling to mind the shrill sound of rats scuttling in the dark. I cast the light of my newly-lit candle to the floor and was relieved to see the floor was bare, but the shadows of the light danced wildly on the wall.

At the top of the stairs, Ainsford took the lead, showing me to the room at the back of the house; the door hanging limply from its hinges in the rotted woodwork. Ainsford pushed the door open and we stepped into the little room. Though our man may have been of diminutive size, our combined mass still engulfed the little room. There was nothing else to be seen in the space, save for the torn wallpaper hanging in places from the aged walls. As I cast my glance around the room, I was suddenly struck by a disturbing fact: that same wallpaper had not begun to peel from old age. Instead, it had been ripped, torn from the wall by a set of powerful hands. What manner of creature was it that had done this thing, I wondered. This room had hardly been the nursery that Ainsford had taken it to be. Instead, this chamber of horrors conjured up images of some madman trapped in this veritable prison. I was turning to say so to our man, when I found myself confronted by a haunting sight.

Ainsford stood in the center of the room, the light from his candle illuminating his strange little egg-shaped head. Yet, in the guttering flame of his light, his curious face had suddenly taken on a more fearful aspect. His eyes, no longer fearful, were staring at me with a kind of malignant glee. I realized only too late that this room was a trap for no one other than myself.

Wordlessly, Ainsford held out an open palm.

"Your revolver, Dr. Watson," he said.

"What is the meaning of –"

"Your gun," he said again, his tone dark and unwavering. I resisted for another moment at which point he added, "I *can* kill you with my bare hands if I must. I was not fortunate enough to have a gun to use on poor Cedric."

"You," I breathed. "You killed your brother."

"And I shall have no compunction in killing you too, Doctor," he said. "Your gun."

I eased the Webley from my breast pocket and laid it out on the table. Ainsford scooped it up and trained the barrel straight at my heart.

"Seeing that our present positions are the way they are," he began, "I would advise you to do as I say, Doctor. There is – or at least there should be – a great deal of money hidden somewhere in this room. The ritual's instructions said as much. My efforts at finding it were crude at best." Here, Ainsford gestured to the torn paper around us. "There are only so many hiding spots in this little room, and I fear that its secret has bested even me. Mr. Holmes spoke of your vivacity in matters of this kind. So, let us see if he spoke the truth."

"And what if I cannot find this treasure you seek?"

"Then I kill you too," Ainsford said. His thumb pulled back the hammer of the revolver. "Tonight," he purred, "of all nights one can *easily* dispose of a body."

My eyes darted around the little room. Surely the task was impossible. There was nowhere to hide anything in a space so mean, so small. I pleaded with Ainsford to see that this was the truth. He shook his head and clicked his tongue like a displeased parent.

"That is a lame and impotent excuse for your lack of trying, Doctor. Surely Mr. Holmes keeps you around for something more than simply marveling at his brilliance. Your carelessness in this case would suggest otherwise."

"Look here," I said, the blood beginning to boil in my veins despite the danger in which I found myself, "the family empire...it can be yours someday. Surely you shall be a rich man soon enough?"

"I have never had a head for business," Ainsford exclaimed. "Surely my father was ever so pleased to pass on this legacy to Cedric simply because – despite being the younger son – he was the one who was going to make something of himself. I have always been one of those idlers and loungers for which this city has been known." A strange smile touched his lips. "Comparatively speaking, you see, this scheme has been much simpler than waiting and working like an honest man."

"You're mad," I spat derisively.

"And with an attitude like that, you'll be dead."

What happened next occurred with incredible speed and violence that I had no idea it was happening until it was very nearly over. Out of the corner of my eye I perceived a dark figure in the doorway to the little room. In a flash, it had sprang into the room and was upon Ainsford before the little man could do anything. As I watched with dumbstruck eyes, I saw that the dark figure was none other than the beggar who had tried to seize my purse in the street. The beggar had pinned Ainsford to the floor, his grimy hands working to wrench my revolver from the man's grasp. The little man fought back but the apparition was quicker and stronger and quickly pulled the weapon from Ainsford's hand. Then he hauled the man to his feet, training the gun directly at him.

"You needn't worry anymore, Doctor," the beggar said in a familiar voice. "I rather think that this whole situation is very much under control."

"Holmes!" I cried. "Thank god!"

"I should never dream of sending you out into the night with a man as patently guilty as Mr. Edmund Ainsford. Come, let us get back this blackguard out into the street. I daresay the authorities shall be pleased to lay their hands on you."

Holmes jabbed the barrel of the gun into the small of Ainsford's back and pushed him out of the room. The three of us descended the stairs and stepped out into the road. To my amazement, the empty alleyway on which we had stood earlier was now crowded with uniformed officers and, standing in the direct center of this group was the familiar figure of Tobias Gregson.

"This is your man, Gregson," said Holmes pushing Ainsford into the Inspector's grasp. I watched with great satisfaction as Gregson clapped irons over the little man's wrists. "You shall be happy to hear, Inspector, that you may charge Mr. Ainsford not only with the murder of his brother but with the murder of Adrian Crawley as well."

"Bless my soul!" the Inspector breathed. "You must be joking, Mr. Holmes."

"I couldn't be more serious, Gregson. I am aware of the lateness of the hour, but I know how diligently you have been pursuing this case, so perhaps you would care to come back to Baker Street to hear the matter through. I am sure that the good Doctor here would not pass up a drink right about now."

After the ordeal of the evening, I was very glad to be back in Baker Street. Drinks had been poured and Holmes had offered Inspector Gregson a cigar which he graciously accepted. Once Holmes had slipped into his chair, and filled his pipe from the Persian slipper, he began his discourse, first filling in the details of our meeting with Ainsford that night.

"If it were not for the man's hubris, I am afraid that I might not have been put on the right track. Ainsford could not help but mention that his brother had disappeared in a room locked from within. It simply could not have been a coincidence that *two* such impossible events as Cedric Ainsford's disappearance and the murder of Adrian Crawley occurred in such swift succession. With my suspicions aroused, I began to reevaluate both cases. Surely the tale that Ainsford was spinning for Watson and I in this very room was nothing more than the bait to get me out of this room and help him in finding whatever treasure he believed was hidden in that house."

"But how could he have known the details of the ritual?"

"You recall that Ainsford told us that the instructions to Cedric were written up by his late father and entrusted into the care of the family solicitor. It was something of a leap in logic – but a fruitful one nonetheless – when I supposed that a family as prosperous as the Ainsfords would elect to be represented by a man as powerful as Adrian Crawley. After you had left, Watson, I cabled Gregson for a complete list of Crawley's clients. Sure enough, the Ainsfords were front and center on that list.

"Ainsford always meant to take his brother's inheritance, so he set his plan into motion. First, he would have to glean the details of the ritual and, to do that, he needed to see the ritual for himself. He sought an audience with Crawley and then killed him; no doubt committing the act *before* he placed the dead man's body in the study. The impossible element of the case would, no doubt, cast a simple murder case in a much more shadowy light. You gentlemen should know that there is no great difficulty in locking a door from outside of the room with the use of a length of string or a bit of wire. Ainsford was no skilled criminal; he was simply a greedy blighter and, despite his best intentions, his crimes screamed of amateur theatrics.

"Let us return then to tonight: Ainsford, now knowing full well what the ritual will entail, accompanies his brother to the house in Wapping. He ensures they are abandoned by their cabbie – no self-respecting cabman would turn up his nose at the fare Cedric promised – and then follows his brother into the building. He needn't worry about leaving footprints in the dust for the tale that he will tell to us accounts for them. He follows his brother to the upstairs room and, together, they strip the room of its wallpaper, certain that they would find the loot hidden in the walls."

"But what is it they were looking for?"

"Surely the Ainsford brothers suspected that their father had returned some of the gold he was rumored to have found in Australia somewhere in that derelict house. Edmund Ainsford was so convinced that he would find it there – and that he simply hadn't done a good enough job looking – that he went so far as to seek me out to do the searching for him. Of course, when I realized what it was that Ainsford was really up to, I sent Watson in my place so that I might observe unseen. My suspicions of the man were confirmed when, after giving him a coin to present to any reluctant cabdriver, I observed him – even at a distance and through the fog – pocket the coin instead of handing it over to his driver. Once the two of you had quit Baker Street, I flew into action, sending off that telegram, urging Gregson and his men to meet me in Wapping. I then fashioned together my crude disguise and raced out into the night after you."

"Crude disguise? You certainly fooled me, Holmes."

My companion waved his hand dismissively. "My charade played its part and, at least, took me to the scene ahead of the officials. Gregson, of course, confirmed my suspicions. All that was left was to make my dramatic entrance at the proper time."

"An amazing piece of work, Mr. Holmes," Gregson said. "The boys at the Yard will be most pleased to have Adrian Crawley's murderer locked up. We've been pulling out our hair for days now…as you know."

Holmes smiled knowingly. "I am glad that I could be of service to you, Inspector. Now then, if you do not mind, the hour is late and I am tired. I am sure that Watson would not mind a good night's sleep after this day."

We bade farewell to the police official and, it was only after I had begun to undo my tie and make for the stairs up to my own chamber, when I was reminded of something. I turned on my heel and strode back into the sitting room where Holmes was still seated, gazing deeply into the fire.

"There is one point you have not explained, Holmes: what did happen to Cedric Ainsford?"

Holmes turned his hawk-like head toward me, his face long, his eyes forlorn. "You heard Ainsford himself explain it. 'Tonight of all nights one can easily dispose of a body.'" I confess that I stared blankly at my friend. He murmured reverently: "Remember, remember the fifth of November…"

"*The bonfires*," I breathed. "Good lord."

"No doubt after killing his brother, Edmund Ainsford made good use of the trunk that he had brought with him, its tell-tale marks left in the front room. He dressed the body in the clothes of a dummy and then, for all the world to see, marched it to the nearest bonfire and pitched it onto the flames."

I felt my skin crawl just at the very thought. "You have told Gregson, I am sure?"

"His men are in the task of searching through what is left of the bonfires nearest to the street in Wapping."

"And the treasure? There was none?"

"It is one of life's ironies, my dear Watson, that if Ainsford had stopped to look at another of the documents that Adrian Crawley had pertaining to his family, he should have found a deed to that seemingly derelict dwelling purporting the property to be worth in excess of a quarter-of-a-million pounds. The coastal soil of the Thames, I am told, is quite a commodity."

Holmes wished me well and I turned to go. I stopped only once more, turning my head and casting a glance back at my companion as he stared blankly into the dancing flames.

The Giant Rat of Sumatra

Originally Published in The MX Book of New Sherlock Holmes Stories: Part XII

Life is infinitely stranger than anything the mind of man could invent, Sherlock Holmes once remarked. Both my friend's chosen profession and an inherent predilection towards the bizarre proved his point to be an accurate one almost every day of the many years which we spent together, yet I can think of no better way to introduce the tale which I am about to tell than by referencing the detective's words. Never, I must admit, have I ever encountered a problem in my life quite so unbelievable and grotesque as the one I am about to relate that, for many years, I deemed it a story for which the reading public at large would never believe. Perhaps in setting down the account to paper I am being too presumptuous, I tell myself even now, and maybe it would be for the best if this most singular adventure never did see the light of day.

It all began in that prestigious year of 1895, a span of twelve months which found Sherlock Holmes in more demand than ever before. There were few days when my friend was not roused from his bed early in the morning by a caller upon the doorstep, and there were even fewer evenings where we both found ourselves sitting idly by the fire of 221b Baker Street. At the beginning of this particular tale, Holmes and I had been called away from London all together to the seaside to investigate a series of seemingly unexplainable goings-on at Whitby Abbey. The case proved to have a completely benign explanation and I feared Holmes may have resented being called away from the city, but he was in a good humor that evening as we sat across from each other in our hotel room, blissfully unaware of what was to come.

The following morning, Holmes and I both rose early with the intent on taking the first train back to London. Despite my friend's mild protestations, I cajoled him to break his fast knowing that the long train ride would be an arduous one on an empty stomach and as we sat together sipping from freshly brewed tea and indulging in some delightful home-made marmalade (courtesy of the innkeeper's wife), I suddenly took notice of a young man rushing up the path towards the inn. He was dressed in the attire of a priest, but I was unable to make out much about him until he bustled into the dining room of the lobby, wringing his hands and speaking in hushed, conspiratorial tones to the innkeeper. I saw the man point in our direction and before I even had time to warn Holmes – who was surely watching the scene play out with just as much interest as me – the young priest was upon us.

"Mr. Sherlock Holmes?"

"That would be me," my friend replied courteously, "but I am afraid that now you have the advantage of me."

Holmes gestured for the young man to take the empty seat beside him which he took only too readily.

"My name is Father Michael Frobisher," he began, "and I come in desperate need of your help. The local police have already begun an investigation, but when I learned that Mr. Sherlock Holmes, the great detective himself, was in town, I simply could not pass up the chance to come to you. Something ghastly has happened, Mr. Holmes, something I can only suspect that the devil had a hand in."

"Then I should imagine that you would be far more able than I to handle such a situation," Holmes replied.

"Oh, you must forgive my poetic license," Father Frobisher replied. "However you must not underestimate the severity of this state of affairs, sir. I believe you to be the only man on earth who can help us."

Holmes flashed a knowing grin. "Then, pray, lay all of the facts before me, Father, and omit nothing no matter how insignificant they may seem."

The young priest sat upright and adjusted the delicate pince-nez which were clipped to the end of his pointed nose. "Simply put, Mr. Holmes, it is murder. Two men of this community – a thoroughly disreputable lot by the name of the Connolly twins – were found murdered this morning, savaged by a hand which cannot be entirely human. I know this only as I am unfortunate enough to be the man to have found their bodies."

The color drained from Father Frobisher's face and I pushed a cup of tea in his direction. He accepted with a thankful smile.

"I do not wish to speak ill of the dead," he continued, "but the Connolly's were not well-revered. It was well-known that they could be paid off to commit any sort of indiscretion, so it was little surprise that they were discovered within the church's cemetery. They appeared to have been killed in the midst of attempting to desecrate a grave."

Holmes's ears perked up at such a detail and he leaned forward on the table, all the better to absorb all the facts of Father Frobisher's story.

"Whose grave?"

"That of the late Charles Morrison, the shipping magnate who died a little less than a month ago."

"Aside from the obvious signs of violence upon their bodies, what else did the scene yield?"

Frobisher shook his head. "I am afraid that I cannot say with any certainty. After I reported to the police what had happened and answered their questions as best I could, they sent me on my way. I confess that I do have something of a reputation for being a busybody in town, and I suspect that the authorities thought of me only as a burden to their investigation."

Holmes considered for a moment. "Clarify one point for me, Father: when you say that the two men were *savaged by a hand which cannot be entirely human*, what, precisely, do you mean?"

Frobisher drew in a deep breath. "Both of the Connolly's – Edwin and Jeffrey – had had their throats torn out. On their faces were looks of extreme terror which I have never seen in another man alive or dead. Something perhaps too ghastly to contemplate killed the two men, worrying them like a wild animal."

"Perhaps it *was* a wild animal," I suggested. "One hears tales nowadays of wolves being spotted in parts of England and Wales. Perhaps the Connolly twins, faced with such a creature, fell victim to its unfamiliarity with human beings."

"A sound theory, Watson," Holmes replied, "and one to which I shall return as we progress." Turning back to the priest, Holmes added, "I shall do all in my power to bring this matter to a close, Father Frobisher. I greatly appreciate your bringing this ghoulish business to my attention and in such a timely manner too. Perhaps you can provide me with the name of your local inspector?"

"The man assigned to the case this morning was Inspector Seward," Frobisher replied.

"Excellent," the detective answered. "I shall seek him out as soon as we conclude here. Before we go, however, I should like to return to the matter of the grave. You say that Charles Morrison died less than a month ago?"

I was unsurprised by Holmes's ignorance on the matter for he had been consumed with a perplexing case at the time that the magnate's death had reached the headlines. Morrison had done more than any man in English history to single-handedly perpetuate trade between Great Britain and the island of Sumatra and it was estimated that over a quarter of all teas, coffees, and spices imported from the island were through Morrison's shipping company. His death had been a severe blow to the morale of the caste of society who inhabited Morrison's sphere, but much was made of the fact that his two sons, Archibald and Nicholas were on hand to carry on his legacy.

In response to Holmes's question, Frobisher nodded wordlessly.

"Can you think of any reason that the Connolly twins should wish to rob his grave in particular?"

"It's relative freshness?" I suggested. "Burke and Hare, after all, robbed graves to supply to medical schools for dissection. I am happy to say that the state of things is different now and lecturers are not required to seek the *services* of resurrectionists, but one nevertheless hears horror stories."

"Is Morrison's the most recently dug grave in the cemetery?" Holmes asked.

"An elderly woman, Mrs. Hoffman, died less than a week ago and was buried on Monday last," Frobisher replied.

"Then I am afraid that that disproves the Doctor's theory," Holmes mused aloud. He tapped his long index finger to his lips in a moment of concentration before he abruptly stood, shrugging on his coat. "I am afraid that we shall yield nothing sitting here, gentlemen. Come, let us return to the cemetery and see what we can glean from there."

We made our way outside, I am sure cutting a set of peculiar figures along the way with Holmes leading us through the streets of the ancient seaside city, the young priest at his side, and I following them closely behind. The morning had taken a turn for the cold and though the sun hung in the sky, its beams doing their utmost to penetrate the grey clouds which worked to blot it out, I still felt a shiver pass up and down my body. Holmes, as usual, seemed to pay the cold no heed and pressed on with Father Frobisher instructing him where to go along the way. We had soon left the town itself and made for a hilly, stone crag on top of which was perched the church. Father Frobisher led us up a narrow stone staircase towards the church, and then pointed towards the small gathering of headstones which formed the cemetery.

Had the markers of the graves not been visible to us, we would have still known that something was amiss. A group of men – two uniformed constables and an inspector dressed in a greatcoat – stood together deep in conversation. The Inspector looked up perceiving our approach and visibly rolled his eyes at the approach of Father Frobisher.

"I thought we told you that we did not need any further insistence, Father," the Inspector remarked coldly.

"Yes, yes," Father Frobisher replied nervously, wringing his hands in his habitual manner, "be that as it may, but I had word that Sherlock Holmes and Dr. Watson were staying at the inn in town and I figured –"

The Inspector silenced the priest with a look. He then turned to Holmes and I. "You gentlemen are Sherlock Holmes and Dr. Watson?"

"Indeed," Holmes replied with a polite tip of his hat. "And if Father Frobisher is to be believed – and I do not doubt his word – you would be Inspector Seward."

"Yes," the Inspector replied gruffly. "As exciting as it is to meet you, Mr. Holmes – we here are admirers of Dr.

Watson's accounts of your work – I do not believe that your assistance is necessary in this matter."

"How do you explain the gruesome deaths of the Connolly twins, then?" I asked.

"Though it chills my blood to suggest such a thing," Inspector Seward began, "I am of the opinion that the Connolly's were joined by a third confederate in their grave-robbing expedition. A disagreement between this third party and the brothers broke out and the third man killed them and escaped."

"This disagreement that arose between the twins and their cold-blooded accomplice," Holmes began, "what did it concern?"

Seward stammered. "Money, certainly," he replied. "What else are most disagreements about?"

"It is then your opinion that the Connolly's were employed by someone to dig up graves in order to supply a specimen for some other purpose? Perhaps, as Dr. Watson suggested this morning, they were employed by a member of the medical fraternity to supply a cadaver for dissection?"

"That is precisely my supposition," Inspector Seward replied. "This third man was obviously far more unhinged than either of the twins suspected and, when they could not agree on a manner to distribute their earnings from this illegal task, he turned on them and killed them."

Holmes stared at the ground and considered for a moment. "Your theory is a sound one, Inspector," he said at length. I arched an eyebrow at how readily Holmes was willing to accept the Inspector's theory, especially as I almost discounted it outright earlier that morning. "Do you have any leads on finding this man?"

Seward smirked. "We have our methods, Mr. Holmes. I shall spend much of the day questioning doctors at the local hospital."

"But what need would they have for cadavers?" I interrupted.

Holmes silenced me. "Watson, please. Inspector Seward's theory holds water for the time being. I should very much like to hear of his progress throughout the day if he feels so inclined."

"Should you wish it, I would be happy to keep you abreast of developments."

"In the meantime," Holmes replied, "would you and your officers be averse to me acquainting myself with the ground for a more thorough examination?"

Inspector Seward shrugged his shoulders. "I don't see why not. We do have to be going, so if you do not mind –"

"Please, do not allow me to detain you any further, Inspector."

Cordially, Holmes extended a hand and shook the Inspector's warmly. Once the three representatives of the law had disappeared, my companion turned to Father Frobisher and dismissed him with a few polite words. Left alone, Sherlock Holmes burst into laughter – an act I found rather distasteful considering our current surroundings.

"What could possibly be so amusing?!"

"I do not know how much longer I could act the part of the unknowing fool," the detective replied. "I was sure from the instant that I saw the Inspector standing over-confidently before his constables that he could not be more in the dark. However, I wished to institute myself into his good graces so he might leave us be and we could gather some actual data. I do hope, my dear fellow, that you did not take too much umbrage with me silencing you as quickly as I did."

I waved away the notion. Then, crouching down, Holmes withdrew his convex lens from his inner pockets and scanned the ground in our immediate vicinity. He moved, carefully, towards the grave of Charles Morrison, his eye to the lens at all times. Once he was before the grave, he sprawled himself out on his stomach, sifting his long, dexterous fingers through the soft dirt and grass. He did this for perhaps five minutes or more before he returned to a kneeling position, fished inside his coat pocket and withdrew a small envelope. He then plucked something off the ground and placed it inside the envelope, wordlessly returning it to its original place next to his breast.

"Well?"

"It is a starting point," Holmes cryptically replied. "I should like to make directly for the morgue and, using our good graces with the Inspector as a skeleton key, examine the bodies of the Connolly twins."

The constabulary was located in a small, stone structure off the main thoroughfare, and once inside, Holmes dropped the name of the Inspector to the desk sergeant who sat just within the building's front door. Stretching the truth to its extreme, Holmes said that we had come on Seward's behalf to make an examination of the bodies of Edwin and Jeffrey Connolly. The desk sergeant led us – at first with trepidation – towards the back of the building to a low, tiled room which served as a place for the dead. Laid out on two identical slabs were the identical figures of the Connolly brothers who, I am sure, led similar lives and died similar deaths.

Both men were of average height and build with flaxen hair. Their pale corpses were scored with deep wounds just as Father Frobisher had said; their throats having sustained the majority of the violence. It was a sorry sight, indeed, and even if the twins had had a reputation of little repute within the town, such grim ends were most certainly not warranted. Holmes and I approached them with some reverence, I leaning over them to make a cursory examination of their wounds. It did not take me long to make a startling pronouncement:

"Inspector Seward could not be further off the mark. No man could have inflicted these wounds, Holmes. These scratches look more like claw marks than anything else."

However, Holmes seemed to have taken little notice of my words. He was instead focusing all of his attention on the dead man's fingernails. He wordlessly went about a minute examination of both dead mans' hands before straightening himself with a self-satisfied smirk.

"Claw marks you say?" he asked, seemingly only half interested. "Your theory of a wild wolf does seem plausible then, does it not?"

"Perhaps," I said, "but I am surprised at you, Holmes. Surely you would normally scold me for theorizing before I am in possession of all the facts. Is that not your maxim?"

"It is," Holmes replied. "However, at present, I must admit that my mind is preoccupied. The manner of the Connolly twins' deaths is only of secondary importance right now."

"Oh? And what is of *primary importance*, then?"

"Charles Morrison," Holmes replied. He extracted his watch from his waistcoat pocket and scrutinized it. "Ah, just as I suspected: we have missed our train for London. Well, if we are to be stuck here for a few hours more, then there should be nothing preventing us from calling on the new patriarch of the Morrison household. Come, let us hail a cab and have a few words with Mr. Archibald Morrison."

*

The home of the Morrison family was by far the grandest on the seaside; a three-story stone edifice with vines of ivy adhering to its aged exterior. It was the kind of house which I knew, as our cab rattled up the gravel drive towards it, had a history. The nature of that history was lost to me, but there was an inherent romanticism in the place which excited me. Sherlock Holmes on the other hand seemed to take no notice of the structure which looked as if it had been plucked from an earlier century and placed where it now stood. Beneath the brim of his ear-flapped traveling cap, his inscrutable grey eyes were set with their customary determination, and he was drumming his fingers restlessly upon his knee. Our cab rattled to a halt and we approached the grand double-doors beneath an ornate portico. No sooner had we made to ring the bell, however, was the door opened from within and we stood face-to-face with a young man who smiled nervously at us.

"Can I help you, gentlemen?"

"Mr. Nicholas Morrison, I presume?" Holmes said.

The young man was utterly taken aback.

"Yes. But…how did you –"

"That is beside the point. My name is Sherlock Holmes and this is my friend and colleague, Dr. Watson. We would like to have a few words with you and your brother."

Nicholas Morrison breathed heavily. "Is this about that unfortunate matter at the cemetery this morning? Archie and I were informed by Inspector Seward only a few hours ago."

"Yes, Mr. Morrison. I do believe that you and your brother could be quite useful in helping Mr. Holmes and I sort this matter out," I replied.

Morrison opened the door wider for us and we stepped inside. He divested us of our hats and coats.

"Do forgive the informality," he said, laying our garments on an ornate chest within the foyer, "but we have recently lost our housekeeper and servant of many years a few days ago. Archie and I have been quite lost these last few weeks without them."

"You have not been burdened with further grievances?" I asked.

"Oh, no," Morrison replied. "However, they turned in their notices a few days before my father's death. But, please, come in. I believe Archie is handling some business in the study."

We crossed a polished marble floor deeper into the house, past a sprawling sitting room, and into a wide-open room overflowing with books. Seated behind a large desk crowded with ledgers and papers was a young man bearing the familial resemblance to Nicholas Morrison. He was a few years older than Nicholas, his temples having already begun to gray, and there was something haughty about his demeanor which was not reflected in the countenance of the younger Morrison son. This man, who I took to be Archibald Morrison, was engrossed in the contents of the papers spread out on the desk as he puffed contentedly upon a pipe.

"Archie," announced Nicholas, "we have guests."

Archibald Morrison peered up at us and arched an eyebrow. "Who are these men?"

"Sherlock Holmes and Dr. Watson," Nicholas replied. "They're here about the tragedy in the cemetery this morning."

"We have already told that numb-skull inspector everything there is to know," Archibald Morrison retorted. "Besides, what could we know about any of this? Father's grave was untouched and that is the only help that we can be."

"I beg to differ on that point," Holmes said. He stepped further into the room, his hawk-like head shifting from side to side taking in the chamber with his habitual penetrating, all-seeing gaze. "For instance, perhaps you could tell the Doctor and I why anyone should wish to desecrate your father's grave."

"How should I know that?" Archibald Morrison returned his attention to the papers on his desk. "Now, if you will excuse me, gentlemen, I am extremely busy this morning and, though I would be happy to help you with your investigation, there is little that I can assist you with. Nicholas, on their way out, please apologize to Mr. Holmes and Dr. Watson that we could not be of more help to them."

And with that Archibald Morrison returned his attention entirely to the work on his desk. Muttering a curt thanks, Holmes turned and walked out of the room. Nicholas Morrison and I found him standing in the hallway outside the study examining an oil painting hanging upon the wall.

"This is, of course, an original?" he said turning to us as we approached.

"Yes. My father was a great appreciator of art. A number by that artist can be found throughout our home. And

I do apologize on my brother's behalf, Mr. Holmes. His rude behavior was not warranted, but he has been under a great deal of stress of late. Our father's death pushed the responsibility onto Archie's shoulders quite suddenly and though he spent many an hour at my father's side in that study learning his business practices, surely those hours alone were not enough."

"Your brother's predicament is an understandable one," I remarked.

"What was your brother doing when we interrupted him?"

"It appeared as though he was going over a record of the latest imported cargo. Only last evening one of our trading ships – *The Matilda Briggs* from Sumatra – put into port. Onboard were crates full of spices, teas, and coffees."

"Sumatra is one of your most frequent suppliers, are they not?" Holmes asked.

"Oh, indeed!" Morrison replied, his eyes twinkling. "Some say that my father opened trade with that country by himself."

"Quite an accomplishment." Holmes returned his attention to the painting and then suddenly spun around on his heel. "Dr. Watson and I must be taking our leave, but you have been very helpful, Mr. Morrison."

So saying, my companion strode off leaving me to apologize for his curious behavior. I caught up with Holmes outside as he was shrugging on his Inverness and starting down the gravel drive on foot.

"I do not understand you at times," I said as I fell into step alongside him. "This morning we are handed a case in which two men are brutally murdered and you regard it with only passing interest, yet you find the machinations of a family – who seem to be only tangentially related to the case – to be of the utmost importance. You know something that I do not, Holmes."

Sherlock Holmes smiled knowingly. Instead of answering me directly, he said cryptically: "You know of my habit of eliminating from my mind all manner of thoughts, fancies, and facts which I do not deem relevant?"

"Yes," I retorted, "like how the Earth revolves around the sun!"

Holmes silenced me with a wave of his hand. "There are times, however, when something will stick to my mental fly paper and simply will not yield. I am suffering from just such a preoccupation now and if I am correct, this matter shall hold unexpected surprises for us both."

I took a hold of Holmes's sleeve stopping him. "What do you mean?" I asked gravely.

"Something of which men of science have only just begun to probe may be inextricably linked to both the death of the Connolly twins and the Morrison family. I have an idea of what we seek, but I must pursue a few arcane zoological texts in order to prove my hypothesis. I fancy that I shall be spending the remainder of the day behind the stacks of the local library."

"And what shall I be doing, then?"

"You, my dear Watson? First, procure for us our rooms at the inn for the rest of the night. We shall not be leaving Whitby before midday on the morrow at the earliest. Then, stop 'round to the telegraph office and wire Lestrade. Tell him to fetch Toby from Pinchin Lane and instruct him to board the first train to the coast as soon as he has done so. We shall be in need of both the dog and his revolver tonight. You too have your revolver?"

"Of course."

"Excellent. After you have carried out those errands, I suggest that you get some rest. It shall be a late night for the three of us and, at the end of it; I fear that we may emerge lesser men because of it."

With these daunting words ringing in my ears, Sherlock Holmes and I parted ways.

I had no idea just how true his premonition of doom was to be.

By two in the morning, the damp chill of the autumn day by the sea had given way to a bone-freezing cold. There was little that I could do other than wrap my great coat around me tighter and massage my fingers through my gloves. I took some solace in the fact that Inspector Lestrade seemed to have been just as perturbed as I by the cold; Holmes however couldn't have cared any less.

Our evening had been one full of activity. After I sent off word to Lestrade at Holmes's request, I heeded his words and returned to the inn where I willed myself to sleep and was only roused when my friend returned from his mission. He told me little of what he had been doing (as was his irritating custom) and insisted that if the Inspector had followed his instructions to the letter that we ought to meet him soon. As we made our way to the Whitby station, the sun was already beginning to disappear over the sea; its orange rays mixing on the water like colors in an artist's pallet. Considering the relative lateness of the hour, it was hardly surprising when few others disembarked alongside Inspector Lestrade from the sparsely populated carriage. He led Toby, somewhat unwillingly, by the leash, and seemed only too happy to turn the animal over to Holmes when he clapped eyes on us. I exchanged a laugh with the little policeman at his words concerning the mercurial Mr. Sherman, Toby's keeper, who threatened Lestrade with bodily harm before he used Holmes's name as a passkey, as I had encountered the exact same scenario when I had first procured the bloodhound some years before.

Our party returned to the inn where Holmes insisted that we eat and, after we had concluded our meal and drained our glasses of port, we returned to our room where we sat in relative silence. It was nearly midnight when Holmes announced that it was time to venture out into the night. From his coat pocket, he produced the small envelope containing whatever he had found at the scene of the twins' murder, and wafted its unseen contents beneath Toby's nose. The dog perked up at the stimulus and broke into an all-out run by the time we hit the street.

I could only marvel at the labyrinth-like path we traversed that night, rushing hither and thither across hilly embankments and up and down flights of steps. At times, it seemed that we were traveling merely in circles, yet Holmes did not seem concerned by the randomness of our journey. If anything, he seemed pleased, murmuring time and time again, "Yes, just as I suspected." Lestrade and I shared a number of curious glances, but we knew that Holmes would only divulge the truth of the matter when he saw fit. In time, we found ourselves at the quayside; the cold intensified as we walked by the docked ships, listening to the water lapping at their hulls. Toby stopped before the moored *Matilda Briggs* and Holmes stopped and considered it for some time before he gave the canine another whiff of his peculiar discovery and we were off again.

We had not ventured far when Toby stopped dead in his tracks and issued a series of savage barks into the night. Holmes stopped too and his pale countenance took on an even greyer pallor as we stood in the light of the moon. Wordlessly, he gestured for Lestrade and me to take up our revolvers. We did so and I felt comforted by the weight of the Webley in my hand; that cold, dead steel giving me some much-needed reassurance as I watched this strange tableau unfold.

"Gentlemen," Holmes whispered, his voice breaking the eerie silence and stillness which had descended over us, "I very much suspect that we are about to encounter something the likes of which we have never seen. Keep your wits about you."

I know that it was not only the cold which sent a shiver down my spine at Holmes's words. I had little time to linger on their potential meaning, however, for Toby began to bark once more – his wails increasing in volume and aggression – and that was when I divined a shape emerging out of the blackness and slowly, stealthily advancing on us.

I could not at first believe what I saw, but as the thing stepped towards us, its form became ever more evident to my unbelieving eyes. I mistook it at first for a dog for it was about the same size as Toby. However, I saw at once that it was much lower to the ground than any canine, and its body was far more elongated and sharper than any dog which I had ever seen. A large, snout-like nose protruded arrow-like from the front of its face, and two beady, black eyes stared at us; their sheen being caught in the light and looking even blacker and more bottomless than I knew they were. As I stared at it longer – in a second which felt like eternity – I realized that this was a creature which I had seen countless times scurrying through the streets of the city but never paid much heed. Yes, I realized, as mad as it seemed this creature was a rat, but of a size that mortal eye had never rested upon.

The giant rat opened its mouth revealing a series of sharp teeth, and the creature issued some kind of snarl which could have emanated just as easily from the depths of hell as it did the back of the beast's throat. Toby unleashed another series of angry barks towards the thing which seemed to break all of us from our dazed reverie. Even Holmes – who I suspected knew full well what we were about to encounter – was rooted to the spot where he stood simply unable to fathom the apparition before us. Toby's fuming outburst must have had much the same effect on the creature itself for it rushed at us. As one, we all jumped back and the creature scurried past us; neither Lestrade nor I having had time to squeeze off a shot at the thing's retreating back.

"Come gentlemen!" Holmes cried after what seemed like another eternity, "We mustn't let it get away!"

I reckon that that night we were all men who were fleet of foot, but the giant rat had the advantage on us; its short, stubby legs inexplicably carrying it faster than we could run. The cold wind biting at my lungs, I felt myself beginning to weaken almost from the start of the chase. However, I knew that I must keep pace with Holmes and the Inspector. I would not allow myself to be blamed for letting the monster – for that is what it truly was – get away.

The next few moments passed by in a daze, but I was next aware of the three of us charging up a frighteningly steep stone staircase; the process seeming to me in the moment to be very much like trying to scale a cliff-face. It was a relief to come to the top of the steps, but we had little time to collect ourselves once more for we were still hot on the heels of the giant rat. Huffing and puffing, we continued after it; my whole chest beginning to burn now, and I felt drops of sweat accumulating on my brow. All at once, I felt my legs give way and I stumbled, collapsing to the ground. Helpless, like a ragdoll, I endeavored to right myself and looked up into the concerned face of Inspector Lestrade who extended a hand to help me to my feet. I looked around and saw that both Holmes and Toby were some yards off; the dog having now fully joined the hunt as much as his master. The over-zealous creature was suddenly out of Holmes's grip, however, and it bounded after the rat and was instantly upon its back. I watched dumbly as the two animals wrestled, clawing at each other; both snarling like feral beasts. I had enough sense to rush forward – exerting all of my remaining strength – and pull my revolver from my pocket, aim, and fire. The bullet met is mark, the giant rat issuing a great gasp of pain as it was wounded. At the sound of the shot, Toby backed away, leaving Lestrade and I to unload round after round into the seemingly undying creature's flank.

The end came quickly for the giant rat and it lulled to one side quite dead. Sherlock Holmes and I collectively heaved a great sigh of relief.

"I still cannot believe my eyes," Lestrade said at length as we stood over the body of the dead creature. "What is it?"

"A true miracle and nothing short of that," Holmes replied. "This oversized rodent – *Coryphomys* – is the largest of its size to have ever lived. I must confess, gentlemen, that even I underestimated its size. I suspected a creature, yes, but something as large and ferocious as this would have gone extinct with the dinosaurs. Its existence is nothing short of truly incredible."

"And this…monster…is what was responsible for the deaths of Edwin and Jeffrey Connolly?"

"Yes, Watson," Holmes replied. "We have brought their murderer to justice, though I never anticipated the toll which doing so would have on all of us. I suspect that I have kept you both in the dark for long enough and I have some explaining to do. Let us retire to the inn and steady our nerves with some drinks. I shall endeavor to lay everything before you both and we shall tend to Toby who I fear is just as shaken as we are."

"But what about the rat, Holmes?" I asked. "We simply cannot leave it here."

Holmes considered. Removing his overcoat, Holmes bundled the beast into it and carried it by himself – how he managed I daresay that I shall never know – once more to the water's edge where he tossed the creature's carcass into the ocean.

"Perhaps it is for the best that the civilized world never knows of the existence of the giant rat of Sumatra. Now, let us be off. It is, after all, exceedingly cold out here."

Half an hour later, we three were thankfully ensconced in the warmth of our room at the inn, sitting comfortably before the fire. We all nursed glasses of brandy while Toby sat curled up in a ball upon the floor, letting the warmth from the dancing flames of the fireplace warm him all over. Holmes downed his drink and lit a cigarette and I perceived that his hand was still not entirely steady after what we had all endured. He smirked at his own jittery fingers, and tossed his match into the fire. He then strode up and down the room in what I thought to be an attempt to regain his composure.

"I admit," he began, "that I was biased from the beginning by Father Michael Frobisher's words when he said that no human hand could have been responsible for the Connolly twins' murder. With that hypothesis in mind, then, I made an examination of the cemetery in which they were found for evidence to support this claim. I was particularly on the lookout for footprints which would have proved that a wild animal was on the loose and the two men were unfortunate to run afoul of the beast. However, I soon found myself out of luck for the Whitby constabulary, it seemed, were just as adept at obliterating evidence as Scotland Yard. No offense to you, Inspector."

"None taken, Mr. Holmes," Lestrade replied, and took a long gulp of his drink.

"However, what I did manage to find proved to be even more helpful."

From the end table at his side, Holmes plucked the small envelope which he had used at the cemetery and for the first time withdrew its unseen contents. In his fingers he held a few tufts of hair.

"I was certain as soon as I found these hairs," Holmes continued, "that it was a wild animal which was responsible for the Connolly's deaths. When Dr. Watson and I made an examination of the two men's corpses in the mortuary, I played a hunch and devoted myself to a study of their fingernails. Just as I had suspected, I found a few strands of the same hair beneath the dead men's fingers. Obviously some kind of struggle had broken out between the twins and their killer.

"From there, my task, gentlemen, was a comparatively simple one. I had read once some years ago of a zoological expedition which was mounted into the darkest jungles of the Sumatran rain forest. In doing so, the men of the team had observed oversized rodents in their natural habit: creatures which modern English society still knows little of. It did not take me long to determine that the hairs which I had discovered at the cemetery belonged to a rodent and, after availing myself to a microscope, was able to conclusively determine the rat's point of origin. However, as I said earlier, I had no idea that the creature would be quite so large. For never considering such an eventuality and subjecting you gentlemen to such a scene, I do apologize."

"Save your apologies, Mr. Holmes," Lestrade said. "The Doctor and I are made of stronger stuff than that."

Holmes nodded in thanks at the Inspector and puffed on his cigarette.

"But, how the devil did the giant rat get to our shores in the first place?" I asked.

"Have you not put two and two together yet, Watson? The giant rat was obviously a stowaway aboard the trading ship, *Matilda Briggs* which put into port from Sumatra on the night of the murders. If I were the Morrison's I would surely reprimand the ship's captain for being careless enough to let such a fearsome, unwanted stowaway aboard in the first place."

"So I suppose that explains your inexplicable fascination with the Morrison family, then?"

"On the contrary, my dear fellow," Holmes responded. "In fact, my approach to this case has been – almost from the beginning – that the real heart of this mystery lies with the Morrison family and that the deaths of the Connolly twins were an unfortunate consequence."

I confessed that Holmes had quite lost me. He responded with another mirthless grin.

"I shall elucidate later, Watson. For now, I suggest that we all attempt to get some sleep. It has been an arduous day for all of us. Tomorrow morning we can bring this business to a successful conclusion."

So saying, Holmes dropped all discussion of the matter. We sat in silence for some time before taking his advice and we all dropped off to sleep; Holmes and I in our beds while Lestrade made do with his armchair before the fire. It was a fitful sleep which greeted me that night, and I was only too glad when the first rays of morning sunshine began to peek through the shutters. I roused myself early, not having to wait long before both Holmes and Lestrade joined me in the inn's front room for breakfast. I could only imagine how much pain Lestrade was made to endure sitting in his armchair all night and asked him as much once he had downed a cup of coffee.

"I have fared better, to say the very least, Doctor."

"I hope that we did not incommode you enough that you will not be able to accompany Watson and me to the Morrison home, Lestrade. I can assure you that your presence there shall make my task a much simpler one."

"I have come this far," Lestrade retorted not without some jollity, "that I might as well see this business through to the end."

Within the hour, we three were making our way up the gravel drive towards the Morrison home once more. Nicholas Morrison greeted us at the door, and drew Holmes aside once we had stepped into the foyer.

"I am afraid that my brother is in just as much of a state today," he said. "You may not wish to disturb him."

"Disturb him, I shall," Holmes rebuked. Wordlessly, my friend bounded off down the corridor towards the study, rapping on the door and hardly giving the room's occupant enough time to answer before he had entered. Lestrade and I bustled in after the detective with Nicholas Morrison following on our heels. Archibald Morrison scowled at Holmes upon our entrance.

"Mr. Sherlock Holmes has returned," he said airily a moment later, "how may I be of service *now*?"

"I would sheath my sarcasm if I were in your position, Mr. Morrison," Holmes said. "I cannot be precise, but I believe that the proper authorities would find grave robbing a hanging offense."

All the color drained from Morrison's face, yet he seemed to regain his composure when he said: "Why tell me this, Mr. Holmes?"

"Your act is wearing thin, Mr. Morrison. I know beyond a shadow of a doubt that it was you who hired the Connolly twins to dig up your father's grave."

"You dare to defame me!" Morrison cried, slamming his fist onto the table. "What gives you the power to walk in here and make such accusations, Mr. Holmes?!"

"Admittedly little right, Mr. Morrison," Holmes replied coolly, "but under the present circumstances – and knowing you as I believe I know you – I can come to no other conclusion. Had your father been the last person to die in the village, I would have been more willing to accept the postulation which said that the Connolly's were employed by someone to rob your father's grave and use his body for some nefarious anatomical purpose. However, any skilled grave robber would have selected the grave of the elderly woman whose death followed your fathers' by a few weeks. Therefore, there must have been another motive behind the attempted grave robbing."

Holmes suddenly turned and posed a question to the younger Morrison: "Mr. Morrison, to the best of your knowledge is there anything missing from this room?"

Nicholas Morrison looked around in his habitual nervous manner. "No," he said, "not that I can notice."

"However I imagine if you had spent more time in this study – as you yourself said that your brother did in the days before your father's death – then you might be even more familiar with its contents. I, myself, noticed the dust atop that safe in the corner of the room when I first entered yesterday afternoon. Clearly, something sat atop that safe for some time until recently. I should wager that it was a case or chest of some kind which your father used for keeping additional money. Perhaps it was even a collection meant especially for you. Am I not correct, Mr. Morrison?"

Archibald Morrison stood fast, unmoving and unspeaking.

"As I see it, then," Holmes continued, "your father knew of your lewd behavior, Mr. Morrison. Yes, I speak to the incident surrounding the resignation of your housekeeper and manservant. I was quite happy to get wind of some local gossip at the public house where your reputation as a cad precedes you, Mr. Morrison. Obviously, your father learned of the true nature for their leaving and as a means of punishment to you instructed that he be buried with that stash of money so you may never get your hands on it. I warrant that he regretted, in the end, the lavish style of living in which he raised you, and was prepared to teach you something of a lesson from beyond the grave.

"Once your father was buried, you discovered what he had done and – being the greedy man you are – took it upon yourself to reclaim the money. You hired the Connolly twins who, for the right price, would be willing to execute any odd job given to them and sent them off to stage the robbing of your father's grave. By a cruel twist of fate, they happened to be in the wrong place at the wrong time and met their fates by one of Mother Nature's most aberrant creations which, ironically, you helped in bringing to this country."

Both Morrison brothers looked to the detective on that last point, but he shut down any of their attempts at questioning him with a stern look. He then left the two Morrison brothers to stare blankly at each other.

"I knew that you were one to stoop low, Archie," Nicholas Morrison said, "but I never suspected that you would do something so…so *horrible*."

"What punishment shall you put to me, Mr. Holmes?" Archibald Morrison asked.

Holmes stared at a spot on the floor and drew in a deep breath. "Considering that you did not actually succeed in robbing the grave or stealing the money, I believe that it is for the best that this incident does not come to light. I am not blind to the importance of the Morrison business, and should your trading company fall so should your solicitors' and other branches of this great business. I would not wish such a fate upon so many for your petulant and dangerous behavior alone, Mr. Morrison."

Archibald Morrison too could hardly make his eyes meet Holmes's. "Thank you, sir."

"I believe, then, that this concludes our business here," Holmes said suddenly. "If the Inspector and the good Doctor and I are to make it to London, we must make haste. We shall show ourselves out, Mr. Morrison."

Once we were outside, leaving the Morrison home behind us, I turned to Holmes and asked: "Shall we not explain this business to Inspector Seward?"

"If we are to tell the Inspector anything, Watson, then let us give him a fabricated version of the truth. He would never believe the reality of this case and if I am quite of the opinion that this is a matter for which the world is not yet prepared."

A Ghost from the Past

Originally Published in Sherlock Holmes - Adventures Beyond the Canon: Part III

During the innumerable occasions in which I have picked up my pen to chronicle one of the adventures of the great detective, my friend and colleague, Mr. Sherlock Holmes, I have never seen occasion to make public the reasons for my friend's sudden retirement from professional life. There were those at the time who considered my friend's decision to give up work as a detective and retire to the countryside as an odd one. He was, after all, rather young to be settling into a tranquil existence on the Sussex Downs, and his decision could not have conflicted with his zealous nature more. I alone know of the reasons which prompted his action and I now have taken it upon myself to make a record of those events – truly one of the darkest hours which Sherlock Holmes and I ever saw together.

My marriage in 1902 took me away once more from 221b Baker Street and by extension my friend and colleague, Mr. Sherlock Holmes, at whose side I had the opportunity to witness firsthand mental acuity truly unrivaled in any other human being. However, there came a distance between the two of us when I took up residence in Queen Anne Street and re-opened my practice, and I do believe that there were times in those days when Holmes ambled about his rooms by himself and quietly resented my actions. I did my utmost to quell these feelings within him, and on the few occasions when I did stop in at Baker Street, I found my friend in singularly good spirits.

It was one evening in the autumn of '03, and I had read of my friend's involvement in no less than four high-profile cases. I decided after finding a particularly heavy rain inhibiting most of my patients to venture out-of-doors that I might shut up my surgery early and pay a visit to Sherlock Holmes. Doing so, I found the deluge had halted all traffic and my journey across the city became an arduous one; I not arriving on my old, familiar doorstep until day had given way to night. I let myself in with my old key which I still habitually kept on my person, and was surprised to find that Mrs. Hudson was not to be found in her kitchenette. I mounted the seventeen steps to our old rooms, and easing open the door found Sherlock Holmes totally absorbed in work at his chemical apparatus. Catching sight of me, he leapt from his seat and clapped me heartily upon the shoulder.

"It does me good to see you, Watson," Holmes said as he gestured for me to take my old seat before the fire just as I had done in the days of old.

"And I you," I replied. I gestured towards his workbench. "You have been keeping yourself occupied?"

"I daresay that I would have been unpleasant company this day," Holmes replied. "I have been busy with my beakers, flasks, and test tubes in pursuit of the truth surrounding a poisoning case in Camberwell. I am very much on my way to finding the solution, but it can wait for the moment."

For some little time we spoke of our present circumstances – Holmes indulging me with tales of his most recent successes, and he in turn pressed me for details on domestic life and my practice. I am sure that he was only feigning interest. But I could tell from the twinkle which resonated in Holmes's perpetually cold, grey eyes that he was simply pleased to see me once more.

"I noticed that Mrs. Hudson is not in," I remarked.

"She has been called away to visit a relative on the coast," Holmes remarked, standing and pouring us two drinks from the sideboard. "Billy, the pageboy, has been quite the useful chap these few days. No less than three times today has he been quite prompt in delivering to me the post. I confess, however, that what with my work with my chemicals that I have neglected it entirely."

"Do not allow me to interrupt you from your routine," I said, settling back in my seat and sipping my libation.

A wry smile broadened across Holmes's usually cruel mouth. "My dear Watson, you are ever the knowing fellow. You intuit on the deepest level and I daresay that even you do not realize when you have done it. Though I am up to my ears in work already, I simply cannot resist the opportunity to take on more. I am like a predatory fish ever in need to water passing through his gills lest he die from lack from stimulation."

Holmes hopped up from his seat and took up the dagger from the mantelpiece and then settled in at the breakfast table where I observed for the first time the none-too-small pile of letters which had been delivered just that day.

"Hmm," Holmes murmured selecting the first envelope, "expensive stationary, written by a woman in her early forties I should imagine. Notice how the envelope has been sealed with gum not a seal. The sender is of a frugal nature, I would wager."

The correspondence obviously did not pique Holmes's interest for he set it aside unopened. He did much the same with half a dozen other letters, making cursory examination of each one before setting it aside with little interest in its contents. He was nearing the bottom of the pile when he stopped, his eyes fixing on a simple, cheap envelope, his name and address scrawled in sloppy script, the ink of the pen having run dry three times in the process of writing out the address.

"This," he said, "is quite unlike the others." Passing me the missive, I examined it minutely.

"Should I apply your methods, I should wager that the letter-writer is on the brink of destitution for the paper and ink suggests that the sender did not have ample material on hand."

Holmes nodded in concurrence as I handed it back to him. He took up the knife and deftly slit the envelope open, a look of concern crossing his gaunt face only once he had done so.

Sherlock Holmes went silent completely.

"Is something the matter?" I asked.

Wordlessly, Holmes held out his palm and turned the envelope upside down. Its contents landed like great leaden blocks in his hand: five orange pips.

"Good lord," I murmured, rising from my seat knowing all too well what this strange message meant. During a case which felt as if it had transpired lifetimes before, Holmes became aware that five orange seeds were used by a number of murderous societies to foretell certain death for one of their members. This message was nothing less than a threat against Holmes's very life.

"There was no return address?" I asked.

"No," Holmes replied. "This particular envelope must have arrived by messenger. In future, I shall instruct Billy to separate which correspondences come by the postman and which do not."

"Who could it be from?"

"I am afraid, Watson, that the list of men and women in this city who would wish to see me dead is one which is none-too-short. It would be nigh impossible to suggest who has sent me this dark message."

Holmes stood, dropping the seeds onto the table and returning to his seat where he plucked his pipe from where it sat on an end table and proceeded to calmly fill it with tobacco from his Persian slipper. I was utterly taken aback by Holmes's nonchalance in the face of the message filled with undisguised malice, that I felt my explosion of complete confusion was justified:

"What will you do?!"

"There is little that I *can* do, Watson," Holmes said gritting his teeth as he tossed aside his used match. "Whoever has an axe to grind with me has taken precautions so that I may never learn his true identity. I shall simply wait. Matters of this variety usually have a way of working themselves out and what I cannot divine I can usually deduce from what will happen very soon."

Holmes's words were confirmed only moments later for we hard an insistent ringing at the bell below. My friend disappeared to answer, and I heard from the hall below his surprised cry at the face of our visitor who stood upon the stoop. I was just as surprised as he when he returned a moment later ushering his informant in the London *demimonde*, Shinwell Johnson, in by the arm.

I have only spoken sparingly in my narratives of Shinwell Johnson, but he became one of my friend's best informants at the turn of the twentieth century. Just as Holmes's own countenance had a manner of opening doors for us in the more respected portions of society, Johnson's had much the same effect in the poorer sections of the city. There were few houses of ill-repute, gambling dens, and hideaways that Johnson was unfamiliar with, and his notoriety in that quarter made him invaluable to Holmes who always asserted that the very best place to hide was in plain view. Who, the detective would ask, would look for an angel amongst a lot of devils? It had been some time since I had clapped eyes upon Shinwell Johnson – the big, broad man looking ever the same as he shuffled into our sitting room – but he looked fearful as Holmes showed him to his seat in a way which I had never glimpsed upon him before. Johnson was built like a pugilist, but now he looked very much like the smallest of men.

"Something has disturbed you?" I queried as Holmes took his customary chair once more.

"Aye, Doctor, something has disturbed me."

Holmes pulled on his pipe, leaning in towards Johnson. "Pray, speak, Johnson, and omit nothing. It must take a great deal to unnerve a man with an iron constitution like yours."

Johnson drew himself up, clearing his throat with some theatricality.

"I was headed home," Johnson began, "making my way up Glasshouse Street, I was, when I noticed a man following me at a distance. He was a tall man, well-built and smartly-dressed, with a long coat and billycock hat, his collar turned up against the cold. I noticed him turning the corner the same time as I did which caught me off guard and he followed me all the way up the road and at the corner of Air Street, I started walking a little faster. I just wanted to see if the bloke would continue to follow me and, sure enough, he does. I'm not a nervous man; you know that, Mr. Holmes, but there was something icy cold about this man which I seemed to detect about him. It's like I had a sixth sense for a moment, and when I still hadn't shaken him, I took off into a full run.

"It was just my luck that the streets were practically empty tonight, so I had an absolute devil of a time trying to lose him. He was a fast man too, and soon he caught up to me. He caught me with a gloved hand which felt like iron when he pressed it into my shoulder and he pulled me into an alleyway. I was kicking and hollering as best I could, but with his other hand he cut off my cries. He pressed me up against the wall of the alleyway and, letting go, I tried to make a break for it when I suddenly felt the point of a knife in my ribs. I looked into his face – his eyes which looked like they were cold with ice – and he snickered with a kind of insane pleasure in what he was doing. Then, deliberately and slowly he reached into his coat and pulled out this."

Johnson reached into his own coat and produced an envelope which looked identical to the one which Holmes had just received. My eyes went wide at the sight, but my friend seemed completely unmoved.

"The man pressed that envelope into my hand and then drawing away the knife, he slipped it back into his own coat, snickered again, and turned on his heel and left me go. I was so rattled by the whole thing that I simply slid down the wall and sat on the ground for what seemed like ages before I could catch my breath. But, you know the queerest part of the whole thing, Mr. Holmes. This here envelope contained nothing but –"

"Five dried orange pips."

"God in heaven," Johnson murmured. "I've seen you do some unbelievable things, Mr. Holmes, but how on earth did you –"

"Because, Johnson, I received an envelope identical to yours with the exact same contents this evening."

"I'm nowhere near as keen as you, Mr. Holmes, but I am no dullard, you can be sure of that. People mistake me for an idiot all the time, but I can assure you that I am as literate as they come. I have read your story, Dr. Watson, about these pips…and how they foretell death. What…what does this all mean?"

Sherlock Holmes was silent for a moment, concentrating on a spot on the floor. "It means that plans for revenge are being enacted. And sooner than I ever would have anticipated."

I stared across at my friend, his cryptic words meaning little to me. "What do you mean?"

Holmes knocked out his pipe and began to refill it, his words seemingly punctuated by his actions. "You both will doubtlessly recall that business of General de Merville's daughter which transpired last September?"

How, I wondered, could I ever possibly forget?

In the days which followed the conclusion of that case, Holmes and I silently agreed to never speak of it for it was of both such a sensitive and disappointing nature that to bring it up would certainly resurrect only too many unhealthy memories. It was in the autumn of 1902 that Holmes was contacted by Sir James Damery who served as the emissary for a client whose illustriousness would have humbled Holmes's not insignificant practice with a request to prevent Violet de Merville from marrying the Baron Gruner, an Austrian nobleman and reputed scoundrel who many claimed was responsible for a whole host of indiscretions; not the least of which was the murder of his previous wife. Holmes was drawn into the case, believing that the only way that Violet de Merville would leave her fiancé was if she had unarguable proof of his misdeeds. In his quest to uncover such material, Holmes called upon the services of Shinwell Johnson who, in turn, brought us into contact with Miss Kitty Winter.

There have been many pitiable souls who have made their way through 221b baker Street, but few I believe were quite as sad as Miss Winter who was so cruelly used at the hands of the Baron that she lost her social position and most of her friends and acquaintances and became like so many unfortunate women in London, forced to walk the streets in an effort to stay alive. She was only too willing to aide Holmes in his mission and informed him in no uncertain terms that the

Baron *collected* women; preserving memories of his indecent rendezvouses with them in a journal which he kept hidden among his possessions. Armed with this new intelligence, Holmes attempted to persuade Miss de Merville to leave her fiancé, but she accused the detective of speaking slanderous untruths about him; his protestations falling upon deaf ears.

It was not long after that the Baron made his boldest move: he attempted to assassinate Holmes, sending two thugs armed with sticks to batter and break my friend. Even from his sickbed, Holmes was determined to get a hold of the book to which Kitty had spoken and elected to use me as a diversion whilst he burgled the Baron's study to retrieve it. I knew little of Holmes's full intentions that night, and I confess that neither of us knew what Kitty had planned, for when Baron Gruner discovered Holmes attempting to make off with his journal, Kitty flew at him with a bottle of vitriol, throwing the acid into his face and leaving him permanently scarred.

In the wake of the violence, the marriage between Baron Adelbert Gruner and Miss Violet de Merville was ended and, though Kitty Winter served a minimal sentence for her violent act, little action was taken against her or my friend for his role in the house-breaking. In the months which followed, we heard nothing from either Kitty or the Baron; their trails having gone completely cold.

And now, a full year later, it seemed that one of them had resurfaced.

"Holmes -" I began, my words catching in my throat before I could vocalize them.

"Yes, Watson," he murmured in response, confirming my worst fears, "I am afraid so."

Shinwell Johnson seemed to have matched our trains of thought. "What are we going to do, Mr. Holmes?"

Holmes considered, pulling on his pipe for what seemed like an hour, still staring hard at a spot on the carpet. "We spring into action, gentlemen," he said at length. "If my darkest fears are true then Miss Kitty Winter is in very much danger. You have kept up communication with the young woman, Johnson?"

"No," Johnson replied. "But it is not hopeless. I think I know where she ought to be. Kitty's a creature of habit."

"That is excellent for us, then, and perhaps deadly for her," Holmes retorted. "If Miss Winter's routine is of a regular nature then our antagonist will surely find her before we do."

"Unless he does not anticipate us to act as quickly as we do," I replied. "Baron Gruner could not possible foresee just how quickly Johnson would come to you."

Holmes managed the ghost of a smile. "You are quite right, Watson. Ever the optimist. However, if we are to do anything, we must act now. I suppose that it would be asking too much of you, Watson, to have your Webley on you?"

"I'm afraid it is locked up at home."

Holmes waved away my words with his hand. "No matter," he said. "We shall manage. Johnson is not squeamish about leaping into the fray and I have a trick or two hidden up my sleeve as well."

Holmes crossed the room and grabbed his stick. Twisting the head, he pulled from its depths a blade which glistened in the light of the crackling fire.

In short order, the three of us had made our way downstairs and out into the street where I was much relieved to find that the rain had dissipated entirely. While Johnson endeavored to hail us a passing four-wheeler, Holmes stood back in the recess of the doorway, his hands thrust into the pockets of his coat, the brim of his hat pulled low over his face.

"You will note," said he under his breath, "that there is a gentleman standing in the doorway of the shop across the way. I cannot speak with any certainty, you understand. But considering our present circumstances, I would wager a good deal he has been assigned to watch our house and our movements."

"Should we not take some precautions," I asked.

Holmes shook his head. "Even at a distance I can tell that he is not armed. That man is no immediate threat, but I fear that once we are gone, he may inform upon our actions to another and we may find our return an unwelcome one."

At that moment, a cab slowed to a stop – the cabbie looking down from his perch at Shinwell Johnson with some contempt which was soon quelled when Holmes and I joined our rather slovenly-looking companion – and climbed into the depths of the carriage. The cabman's hesitation rose yet again when Johnson called out for an address in Soho, and in short order we had set off through the city.

Our party was a quiet one that evening; each of us lost in our own thoughts and fears. Though Holmes would never have vocalized it, I could read true perturbation on his face and he was even whiter-looking than his usual pallor. I ran a hand over my own brow and wondered what kind of mission we had embarked upon. It was not unlike my own experiences during the Afghan campaign; a whole host of nightmares which now seemed like they were a lifetime past. For how long we rattled through the metropolis, I cannot truly say for I did not observe our journey, so lost was I in my own ruminations. When we did alight from the cab, however, we were faced with an inauspicious-looking brick building tucked away on a street which I could not place. Johnson led the way as Holmes and I followed and we approached an old, weathered-looking door. Johnson rapped upon it and we stood in silence for what felt like an eternity.

As we waited, I watched Holmes's nervous eyes darting around him, taking in the whole scene. His body went stiff for a moment and I turned to him, but he shot out an arm, grabbing me by the wrist.

"Do not turn around, Watson," he hissed, "your very life may depend upon it."

Never more did I want to cast aside my friend's warning and see just what he saw, but I knew better than to disobey his command, and a moment later, I heard the sound of a bolt being drawn back from within the door and a very familiar face looking out upon us. The shock of red hair was immediately noticeable, but I do also confess to a sudden feeling of presence within our space; an intangible effervescence which came with the door opening pulled back and the enigmatic Miss Kitty Winter stepping into our lives once more. She registered our faces in turn and was about to speak when Holmes cried out:

"Miss Winter, please get back inside!"

No sooner had Holmes said anything than I was being pushed forward by my friend's iron grip. Johnson followed suit and in the confusion I fell upon my face inside the building. As I tumbled to the ground, the wooden door above me exploded, a thousand tiny splinters cascading over my body. I heard a great commotion from above me and looking up I saw Miss Winter thrust the battered door shut and throw the bolt home sealing us inside. Sitting up, I registered looks of shock on both Miss Winter's countenance as well as Shinwell Johnson's.

"My apologies," Holmes said stepping away from the door. "As soon as we disembarked our own cab, I was certain that we were being followed. As we stood by the door I could make out a hansom in my peripheral vision and was quite certain that I saw the glint of a rifle barrel from within. We have just survived an attempt on all of our lives."

I scrambled to my feet, my heart pounding in my chest.

"What the devil is this all about?" Kitty Winter cried.

"You're in danger, Kitty," Johnson said, stepping forward and taking her hands in his large appendages. "It's…*him.*"

Kitty went silent, seemingly lost in some kind of far-off daze. "Oh, god," she managed at last, "anything but that."

"I am very much afraid to say that Johnson is correct," Holmes replied. "Just today both Johnson and I received threats against our lives. They could only have come from the Baron Gruner."

For an instant, I thought that Kitty was going to be ill, her face going entirely white and her jaws locked together in total fear.

"Is there nothing that I can do to escape that man…that fiend?!" she cried, tears welling up in her eyes.

"You've got nothing to worry about," Johnson said, reassuringly patting her hand, "we're here now. Mr. Holmes is here now."

Kitty defiantly yanked her hand away from him. "What good can you lot do? You tried to stop him last time and he got away. Even then. I am the only one who did anything to stop him from ever being able to hurt anyone ever again. And I do not care one bit if you think that what I did was uncivilized, Mr. Holmes. I may have been a lady once but those days are so long gone now, I can hardly remember the woman I once was. You – and the rest of the law for that matter – may think that what I did was unlawful, but they will never know what Baron Gruner did to me, and they can never convince me that what I did was wrong."

Tears were freely streaming from the young woman's eyes now and I gently proffered her my handkerchief which she rather reluctantly accepted. She dabbed at her tears and worked to catch her breath.

"Kitty," Holmes said tenderly, "I will do everything in my power to prevent Baron Gruner from ever hurting you – or anyone else for that matter – ever again. I have yet to stand in the dock for what I did to bring him to book before, and I very much doubt that I shall ever stand in the dock for what I am to do now."

"What are you going to do?" I asked.

Sherlock Holmes drew in a deep breath. "When Gruner sent me those orange pips he threw down the gauntlet. Had this been another day-in-age that would have been sufficient means to challenge the blackguard to a duel. Though we are living in the time of Edward and not Elizabeth, I see little else that I can do but act accordingly."

"Holmes, you are not seriously planning on going out there and facing him alone?"

Holmes shrugged off my protestation.

"But those men are armed, for heaven's sakes!"

Again, my plea seemed to fall on deaf ears. Holmes approached the door and, unlocking it, opened it wide. I expected – for a moment – to be met with a hail of gunfire, but none came and Holmes silently stepped out into the street. He was beyond my sight now and I waited with baited breath, but was met with only silence – a silence which I could not accept and which chilled me to the core.

I rushed to the open door, ignoring the cry from Johnson and stared out into the street. What I saw I could not rationalize: Holmes stood over the corpse of a man, the hansom cab which had conveyed our would-be assassins here speeding away. I rushed forward to my friend's side, but if I had hoped that a closer look at the scene would reveal anything to me then I was sorely mistaken for I was flummoxed all the more when I caught sight of the dead man sprawled out on the ground before Holmes.

He was dressed in rags which hung loosely over the dead man's physique. I would have suspected that the dead man was once a handsome man, but I saw suddenly that he was horribly disfigured. There was little left of the man's face. Had I not suddenly recognized the dead man, I would have surely suspected that the poor creature was the victim of some horrible, leprous disease and not vitriol.

"Holmes!" I murmured, too astonished to speak.

"My thoughts mirror your own stupefaction, Watson. This is the Baron Adelbert Gruner – the man from whom we have surely been running all evening."

It was not without some effort that Holmes and I carried the Baron's body back inside, laying it on the floor of the low, Spartan room which Kitty Winter called home. Had my mind not been elsewhere, I would have contemplated Miss Winter's continued pitiable state as she sought refuge in such an unwelcoming environment as this. But I was distracted by the corpse which lay at my feet, and surely just as confused as Holmes, Miss Winter, and Shinwell Johnson.

If Holmes was perturbed, however, he did not allow himself to show it for long, before he had knelt down and was examining the clothes of the dead Baron Gruner and scrutinizing him even more closely beneath the glass of his convex lens. It took not take a penetrating gaze, however, to see that the Baron had been stabbed in the heart, his death was surely an instantaneous one. At length, he stood, pocketing his glass, and heaving a deep sigh.

"Anything?" I asked.

"I think so," Holmes replied. "The Baron is dressed in clothes which surely were at one time his own, but which destitution has rendered beyond recognizable. The original tailor's name can still be perceived within the shirt's collar. I should imagine that for some eight months or so, the Baron has been living on the streets alongside the poor of the city."

"How can you say with such a degree of accuracy?"

Holmes knelt down once more, his long, probing fingers darting into the dead man's pocket and pulling out a few sheets of crumbled paper. "Each of these," he said, "belongs to various hostels and soup kitchens designed by some of the more charitable members of the city to help the less fortunate get back on their feet. The oldest of these tickets bears the insignia of 'Penrose and Son,' which was an operation run by one Donald Penrose, the philanthropist whose untimely death happened some eight months ago. Seeing as this is the most crumpled and worn of the lot within the Baron's pocket, I would hazard a guess that it has been on his person the longest.

"The other two belong to similar establishments, the third of which is nearly new. I would wager that that was the Baron's most recent port-of-call."

Holmes passed the scrap of paper to me for examination. It read its simple message aloud: "Dr. Quayle's Home for the Destitute."

"The name is not an unfamiliar one?"

"There are few in these parts who haven't sought refuge under Dr. Quayle's roof at some point in their lives," Kitty said.

"Could we journey there now?"

"I'd imagine that they've shut up for the night, but you have attempted to work wonders before, Mr. Holmes, perhaps you can try yet again."

Holmes flashed the ghost of a grin. "I would be most obliged, Miss Winter, if you accompanied us." Holmes turned to Johnson. "We cannot very well leave a corpse unattended. Would you be willing, Johnson, to run along and fetch Inspector Layton of the Yard? Tell him that I have sent for him expressly. Layton is a stalwart chap who, I believe, will be quite willing to see this matter through with the utmost discretion."

"I shall do just as you ask, Mr. Holmes."

"Excellent," Holmes zealously replied. "Then let us not waste one minute more and stay on the trail while it is still quite hot."

We parted ways; Holmes, Miss Winter and I on foot to find the hostel owned by Dr. Quayle and Johnson off to fetch a cab to take him to Scotland Yard. It was gone ten o'clock by the time that we found ourselves outside the inauspicious doors of Dr. Quayle's residence; a plain-looking stone façade which boasted a double-set of thick, wooden doors. Holmes took hold of an aged knocker and pounded upon the door as though he were seeking entrance to a great castle of old and, after a moment of utter, eerie silence, the door swung open to reveal a broad-shouldered man of middle-age carrying a lantern and attempting to rub the last vestiges of sleep from his eyes.

"What is it?" he inquired his voice even and cool though not without a hint of irritation.

"Dr. Quayle, I presume?" Holmes said. The man nodded in reply. "My name is Sherlock Holmes. I must speak to you right away on a matter of the gravest importance."

Holmes's name seemed to stir something within the Doctor and he opened the door wider for us. I could see that at one time, Dr. Quayle must have been a force to be reckoned with: his broad frame would have certainly fared him well on any rugby team he chose. His face, adorned with a well-tended beard, spoke of the great stress which must have surely drug the poor man down working as he did day-after-day with the most pathetic of London's citizens. He was dressed in a simple, worn jacket, his tie undone around his neck. From the manner in which he held his neck and head, I would have thought that the man had fallen asleep at his desk.

He led the three of us further into the building: a small, claustrophobic dwelling, but I am sure that it was a safe-haven for those who could seek asylum within its walls. We ducked into a small room which served as the doctor's office which was outfitted with a roll-top desk, a worn-looking chaise, and a bookshelf overflowing with texts. Dr. Quayle took a seat at his desk and gestured for us to sit. Holmes refused, but insisted that Miss Winter and I do so.

"Now then, Mr. Sherlock Holmes," Dr. Quayle said, picking up a pipe from his desk and filling it with the utmost concentration, "what is this matter of the gravest importance?"

"I am inquiring after a man," Holmes said cryptically.

"Dozens of men pass through here day after day," Quayle replied, lighting his pipe and easing back in his chair. "You will have to be a bit more specific."

There was something odd about the Doctor's tone. It was almost as though he were fighting us, but his relaxed demeanor and calm countenance seemed to suggest that he was being nothing but open with us.

"He would have been a quite *distinctive* man," Holmes said. "Had you seen him, you would have surely remembered him. He was dressed in clothes which would have at one time been quite expensive, and his face was horribly disfigured."

A light came into Dr. Quayle's eye. "I believe I know the man to whom you refer," he said. "He was quiet man. Kept to himself. I suppose that he felt rather self-conscious about the scars from the vitriol."

"Yes, yes, of course," Holmes said. "But do you know what became of him?"

"He was here this afternoon," Quayle answered. "I remember asking him if I could perhaps do something – about his face, that is. He seemed to shrug off the suggestion. And then he made something of a scene again when he had run out of porridge. He said that he could easily get a cup of soup at another hostel and – for the sake of the others – I tried to avert a scene and suggested that it would be best if he went on his way. I do so hate turning anyone away, but I felt as if there was little else that I could do for him."

"Do you remember where he said that he might go?"

Quayle considered. "Mrs. Notterton's, if memory serves."

Holmes nodded his head in understanding.

"Could you perhaps enlighten me, Mr. Holmes, why you are seeking this man?"

"He is connected with a case which I am currently investigating," Holmes replied. "I have been hoping to put a few questions to him and, if as you suggest that he has gone to Mrs. Notterton's, then I am sure that that is where we shall find him. Hers is one of the premiere establishments of its kind." Holmes considered for a moment. "It is, however, an awfully long walk to that part of town and Dr. Watson, our companion, and I are low on funds to procure a cab. Is there any way that you could find out – for the three of us – if our man is still there?"

Quayle smiled. "As a matter of fact, I do believe that I can do that for you, Mr. Holmes."

The Doctor rose from his seat. "If you will follow me upstairs, I can telephone Mrs. Notterton and find out for certain whether your man is still there."

We rose and followed Dr. Quayle out of his office and towards a cramped staircase which led to the upper story of the building. They were, I surmised, the Doctor's living quarters and he explained as we ascended that he kept the telephone out of sight lest he be accused of hypocrisy for owning such a device while tending to a portion of the city who could only dream of owning one.

Never will I forget what greeted us as we reached the top of the stairs. The room into which we entered was another low and Spartan one, but it was made all the more surprising by its sole occupant: a well-dressed woman who stood poised with a gun in her gloved hand. Sherlock Holmes reached the top step and heaved a great sigh.

"I was beginning to think as much."

"My apologies for the theatrics, Mr. Holmes," the woman said, "but if I remember correctly, you are blessed with a flair for the dramatic as well. Why else would you stage a scene so sensational as coming to my own home, bringing with you the same trollop you have at your side now, and convincing me not to marry the man I loved?"

"I think, Miss de Merville, that my actions were entirely justified."

Violet de Merville's eyes flashed like wildfire. "You do not know the half of what your actions did to me, Mr. Holmes," she said, leveling the gun barrel at the detective's heart. "You have caused me more pain and heartache than you could possibly imagine."

"But we saved you from a fate far worse than death!" Kitty cried.

Violet de Merville suppressed a loud guffaw. "You think you know a fate worse than death? I have seen it before my very eyes. My father…my father was once a strong man. He was a decorated military hero, but he was all but crushed by my courtship to the Baron."

"I very much think that that was your fate," I remarked snidely.

She turned the gun on me. "His torturous existence in those days was a peaceful one compared to the ruin he faced after the Baron was incapacitated, after you and Miss Winter entered my life. The scandal which broke in the days following – the news that his own daughter was very nearly deflowered by that fiend – was simply too much for my father's already crumbling constitution. Day after day, I watched as he would sit in a bath chair before an open window, staring blankly out into the garden and not seeing the garden at all. I vowed revenge in that moment, Mr. Holmes. I vowed revenge upon you, Miss Winter, and the Baron himself for making a laughingstock of my good name and for ruining my father so."

"So all of this," I said, "this has all been your devising?"

"With a little help from Dr. Quayle," Violet retorted. "I cannot overstate how serendipitous these last twenty-four hours have been for me and the good Doctor."

"This hostel would very likely not exist without the generosity of the General," Quayle said. "He has been a family friend for many years and, when I expressed to him my philanthropic aspirations, he was the first to loan me a hefty sum to get this place off the ground. I will always remember him for that one generous action, and that endeared him to me for the rest of my life. This past year, then, has been one of the hardest of my life as I too have watched that great man fall so far. In that time, I have grown close to Violet and harbored with her the same drive for revenge. She told me of the Baron and, after I learned what became of the blackguard, I was determined to help her.

"Violet told me that the Baron was very likely homeless and destitute after the scandal which broke, and so each day I would remain vigilant should anyone matching his description come to the hostel. And then, this morning, it happened. I chanced upon him and knew that I could not possibly let the opportunity go. I spoke nothing but the truth earlier, Mr. Holmes, when I said that the Baron very much caused a scene, but instead of sending him on his way I brought him to this very room and ensnared him like a spider does a fly. I suppose I rather overplayed my narrative when I made mention of the vitriol, did I not?"

"Only someone who knew the identity of the man I was seeking would know how he came by his disfigurement," Holmes said airily. "I knew you were leading us into a trap from that moment on."

"The Doctor telephoned me," Violet de Merville continued, "and I arrived here this evening. I can only begin to describe the look in his eyes when he saw me again, Mr. Holmes. Horror and anger and regret all mixed in his gaze…a look which I cut short very quickly with the aid of the Doctor's surgical knife."

I looked over and saw the very same instrument lying upon Dr. Quayle's desk.

"And then to complete my scheme," Violet continued, "we prepared two envelopes containing orange pips. I knew that I could entice you to take the case with such a dramatic gesture."

"The real difficulty was in tracking down your lackey, Mr. Johnson," Quayle said. "Nevertheless, those who frequent my hostel are not unaware of Mr. Johnson's whereabouts and I was able to find him before the day was out."

"Having delivered the pips to both of you, I was certain that I could lead you both to believe that the Baron was alive and well and out for revenge upon you both. It was then only a matter of following you to Miss Winter's – another action which I clearly foresaw, Mr. Holmes – and from there to Dr. Quayle's. I have been anticipating this moment all evening, and it has finally come."

I watched the hate simmering in Violet de Merville's eyes, and for the first time in many years, I suddenly became aware once more of my own mortality. For a brief instant, I was certain that this was the end of my life – of Holmes's life – and there was little that I could possibly do.

Suddenly, from below, I heard the sound of a door swinging open, followed by two sets of footsteps. Holmes's eyes brightened.

"Unless I am very much mistaken that will be my good friend, Shinwell Johnson, accompanied by Inspector Layton of Scotland Yard who have come to our rescue."

In an instant, Quayle had leapt for his knife. I bounded towards him, rushing to pry the weapon from his grasp. As I did so, I caught a glimpse of Holmes lunging for the firearm in Miss de Merville's hand. I braced myself for the sound of the blast, but none came, and as I managed to wrench the long, thin blade from Dr. Quayle's grip, I turned and saw that Holmes was desperately working to prevent Violet from pressing the gun to her own temple. No sooner had the commotion began than it ended. Shinwell Johnson and a burly Scotland Yard official had lumbered into view at the top of the stairs.

Violet de Merville dropped the gun to the floor with a resounding *thud*.

It was past one in the morning by the time that Sherlock Holmes and I returned to 221b Baker Street. The rain had started to fall from the heavens once more; a tempest which was befitting of our solemn spirits as we sat silently in our armchairs before the fire. Holmes stared into the undulating flames of the fireplace, his face devoid of color. I nursed a brandy, gulping the last of it down, and setting the empty glass upon the table at my side. At length, I sat forward in my chair, drawing in a deep breath.

"I am afraid that I have to go," I murmured.

"You should run along," Holmes replied. "Mrs. Watson will be wondering what has kept you for so long. You shall have quite a tale to tell her come morning."

I managed a half-hearted smile.

"I rather think, Watson," Holmes continued, "that the events of the day have proven something to me."

"Oh? And what's that?"

"That it is time for me to quit. The world is changing, my dear fellow, and I am beginning to see the consequences of my work play out before me."

"You cannot blame yourself for Violet de Merville," I said. "You must remember what Miss Winter said – you saved her from a fate worse than death."

"And consigned her to a year of devoting every hour of her waking life plotting revenge against all those she believed wronged her. I never set out to be a good man, Watson, but surely that is the action of the purely evil – to wrong someone so severely."

I sat stunned by my friend's words.

"Ghosts from my past are becoming quite plentiful of late," he added, his voice barely registering above a whisper.

From a pile of newsprint at his side, he drew out the latest edition of *The Times*. The paper had surely sat unread all day like the post while Holmes labored over his chemicals. He had marked a particular column and, passing me the paper, I saw instantly what had attracted his attention:

Famed American Opera Star Irene Adler, Dead

"Oh, my dear Holmes...I...I'm so sorry."

"You need not worry about me, my dear fellow," Holmes replied. "My mind is quite made up on the matter. I have never given credence to spirits, but when ghosts continually surround us, perhaps it is time that we yield to them. And these particular specters are quite adamant about my retiring. I shall bow to their will."

I knew that there was no use in arguing the matter. Once Sherlock Holmes had set his mind to anything, it would take the Almighty himself to persuade him otherwise.

"Very well," I said at length, my own voice very nearly drowned out by the crackling flames, "then let us enjoy one last opportunity to sit side-by-side in these chairs and remember days gone by – populated as they may be by ghosts from our past."

Sherlock Holmes managed a grin.

"Come," I said, filling my pipe, "I needn't return home quite so soon. Why waste such a perfectly good opportunity for a quiet chat?"

And we certainly did not. We sat for hours in our old, familiar chairs until the fire had long since died away and the sun rose, dispelling the dark memories and long shadows of the day – and so many like it – from our minds.

The Adventure of the Weeping Stone

Originally Published in The MX Book of New Sherlock
Holmes Stories: Part XV

"It's the abominable noise, Watson," said Sherlock Holmes.
"It's been upsetting the bees."

Holmes lifted his gaze from the honeycomb which he
held in hand and addressed me from across the yard. He
slipped the comb back in the apiary, then took up the can of
smoke, and proceeded to pan it across the writhing bodies of
the insects within.

I had expected some of Holmes's attention to be
focused on his bees as I visited him that summer day in 1911,
but I had not anticipated such myopia from my friend.
Frankly, it was frustrating. I had seen very little of Holmes of
late and I had been looking forward to my visit – one which I
had coordinated to the minute detail so that I may not be away
from my practice for too long, and which happened to
coincide with my wife taking a trip into the country of her
own. But now, as I stood in the yard of Holmes' cottage on

the Sussex Downs, I found that the detective seemed to have little interest in my presence. He hadn't even greeted me at the door when I arrived; instead I found, alighting from the trap which had conveyed me thence from the train station on my own, being welcomed to the cottage by the housekeeper. My bags were taken up to my guest room and I was told that Holmes was busy with his bees. As I stepped outside to warmly embrace my friend, I found him barely looking up before he exclaimed that the recent nearby commotion was offensive to his honey-producing acquaintances.

"And it is good to see you too," I grumbled. "I trust that your bees have been keeping you busy?"

"Exceedingly," Holmes said, as he crossed the yard, removing his thick gloves one finger at a time. He had divested himself of his net hat which he cast onto a wooden rocking chair by his side. I looked at my friend's familiar countenance and could not help but feel that time was melting away. Save for a few lines to his gaunt aquiline features, and touches of grey to his temples, Sherlock Holmes looked ever the same. He smiled a knowing grin as though he were able to divine my thoughts – a feat which he had done on more than one occasion – and then gestured for me to sit in the vacant chair opposite his.

"Time has been good to you, my friend," I said as I sat. Holmes waved away the notion with his hand. He reached into the inner pocket of his tweed coat and withdrew his old cigarette case. Passing it across, I lit a cigarette and settled back in my seat, feeling for an instant that we two were once more seated around the fire of 221b Baker Street in London.

"Your practice has been a successful one," Holmes said. "Though I fear that your wife's attention to detail is beginning to wane."

"Whatever do you mean?"

Holmes indicated with a bony finger. "There is a spot of iodine on your right forefinger," he said. "Surely it has resided there since yesterday when you last attended your surgery. Mrs. Watson must have failed to notice it for no wife would allow her husband to go out for so long with such a stain upon his person."

I chuckled. "Your powers have not faltered, my friend. However, my wife has gone on her own trip. She left yesterday afternoon. I saw her off during luncheon."

The housekeeper came with a tray and two glasses of claret. Holmes and I clinked our glasses together. The tableau could not have been a more familiar one.

"Do you miss it much," I asked. "Baker Street, I mean. Working as London's only *unofficial consulting detective?*"

Holmes parted his lips, preparing to speak, when we were arrested once more by the presence of the housekeeper.

"Beg your pardon, Mr. Holmes," she said, "but there is a gentleman to see you in your parlor."

"Are you expecting anyone?" I asked.

"No," Holmes replied. "Did he give you his name?"

The housekeeper handed him a card. Holmes studied it for a moment before passing it across to me. It read: *Dr. David Laramie.*

"His name is a familiar one," I said.

"Yes," Holmes replied. "Dr. Laramie is foreman of the excavation project on the beach below. It is his project which is causing such a commotion and upsetting my bees. Let us see what Dr. Laramie wants from us, Watson, and if nothing else I may complain about the noise."

We found Dr. David Laramie pacing the sitting room as we drew into it. He was a tall, fair-haired man in his early fifties, but was possessed of a youthful expression and physique that I could have easily mistook him for a much younger man. As soon as his eyes fell upon Holmes, he all but rushed across the room to meet him.

"Thank god you were in, Mr. Holmes," he cried. "You are the only man who could possibly help us."

"Please, Dr. Laramie," Holmes said coolly. "Compose yourself. I am prepared to hear through whatever it is that you have to say." Holmes gestured for the man to sit on the settee. Laramie did so.

"This is my friend and colleague, Dr. John Watson," Holmes continued. "Dr. Watson, as you are doubtlessly aware, has been at my side for nearly all of my cases and has drawn up public records of them. I owe something of my celebrity to him."

Laramie flashed me a glance and a quick "how do you do" but he returned his gaze to Holmes. The detective took a seat in his old, familiar velvet-lined armchair which had been a fixture of our sitting room in London for so long, and pressed his hands together in his habitual, contemplative gesture.

"Now then, Dr. Laramie," Holmes said calmly, "what is it that you brings you to me this morning, and who are the '*us*' of whom you speak?"

I knew full well that Holmes knew already the answer to that question. Indeed, there were few households in England that were unaware of Laramie's work in the area. It had been a little over three months since a large rock had been found on the stretch of beach near Holmes's cottage. This unique discovery attracted the attention of one of the larger universities in the country who promptly dispatched a team – led by Laramie – to investigate. In the time since, Laramie and his team had discovered that the large rock appeared to have come from South America. How this rock could have made it onto English shores was a mystery which they had yet to solve, and there were few corners of English academia which hadn't attempted to put forth a solution. On occasion, the papers would carry the latest bit of theorizing – the latest postulation suggested that the rock had been embedded in the cliff face overlooking the beach and had been exposed during a recent collapse; a notion which presented nearly as many questions as it did answers – but it seemed that Laramie and his team of archaeologists were no closer to answering the most tantalizing of questions so often on the lips of interested parties.

When the discovery of the rock had first been made, I made sure to question Holmes on it during our irregular correspondence. He confessed to not being overly interested in the matter. "That is one mystery, my dear Watson," he had written, "which I feel is best left to the others."

How ironic, then, I considered that Holmes should find himself drawn into the business after all.

"My entire team is being questioned by police this morning," Laramie said. "My assistant, Mr. Macaulay, was found dead this morning."

Holmes leaned forward in his seat. "Pray, lay all the facts before me, Dr. Laramie." I could see it in Holmes's cold, grey eyes the thrill of the chase. Like a bloodhound he was once more on the scent.

"Macaulay was discovered on the beach this morning," Laramie reiterated. "He was found not far from the sight of the dig. We have been studying the rock day and night, the area entirely cordoned off. There was no sign of any disturbance to the scene save Macaulay's footprints which were visible in the sand. And yet he is dead, Mr. Holmes.

There are no marks of violence upon his body, but on his face…he looks as if he were frightened to death."

Laramie grasped the knees of his trousers to stop his hands from shaking. "I am not ordinarily an anxious man, Mr. Holmes, but this has unnerved all of the men. There's something devilish in all this."

"Surely there must be some rational explanation," I said, too afraid to admit that I found this man of science's belief in something otherworldly just a little disquieting.

"Ordinarily I would think so too, Dr. Watson," Laramie said, "but our investigation of the rock has born worrying results. There are inscriptions made upon the rock; hieroglyphs whose meaning we cannot divine. However, in comparing notes with a colleague who has made an intensive study of the ancient Inca civilization, we are currently of the belief that this stone may have been a part of ancient, ritualistic sacrifice. And…it would explain the blood."

"Blood?" said Holmes. "I thought you said that Macaulay's body showed no signs of violence."

"That is true," Laramie replied. "However the stone itself. It has been known to weep blood, Mr. Holmes. A number of the men are rightfully afraid. I have ensured that the men have never touched the stone, you understand, but even being in such close proximity to it has felled a few of them on occasion. Men have become quite ill because of that stone. I'm sure of it. There's something unnatural about it, and poor Macaulay's death only proves that fact even further."

Sherlock Holmes considered, tapping a finger to his pursed lips. "When was Macaulay last seen?"

"He was in the company of my daughter, Rebecca, and Mr. Anderson, another researcher, at the Tiger Inn in the village. Macaulay left just before ten o'clock I am told and was not seen for the rest of the night. His body was discovered this morning. As soon as I was made aware, I contacted the police and they have been speaking to all of the men since. I broached the subject of speaking to you with the investigating officer and he begrudgingly allowed me to visit you."

Laramie drew in a deep breath. "Mr. Holmes. You would do much to ease my mind if you were involved in this investigation. Please, please say that you will accompany me back to the dig."

"I shall be happy to help, Dr. Laramie," said Holmes rising from his seat. A rush of relief crossed the man's face.

Turning to me, Holmes said, "You would not be averse to joining me, would you, Watson?"

I said that I should be happy to help in any manner I could.

A few moments later we were seated together in the rear of Laramie's automobile bouncing across the dirt road towards the excavation site.

It was a beautiful summer morning. The sun hung high in the sky, a gentle breeze blew inland from the ocean which stretched out endlessly before us. If we were not on our way to visit the scene of a man's death, I should have taken in the striking vista all the more. However, I was forced to temper my outlook and remind myself that we were currently engaged in solemn business.

Laramie's driver deposited us on the rocks above the beach; a number of wary-looking workman standing and conversing in small groups. At the far end of the beach I could plainly see the mysterious stone; at least five feet in height and standing like a noble sentry upon the sand. Try as I might I could not make out the form of the late Mr. Macaulay upon the beach, and in short order I realized why as an official-looking person advanced towards us.

"Welcome back, Dr. Laramie," he called. Then, catching sight of Holmes, he added, "How nice of you to join us, Mr. Holmes. I confess that I was rather reluctant to bring you in, but this sort of thing seems right up your street."

"My thanks to you, Inspector Mackenzie," Holmes airily replied, toying with the head of his stick as he spoke. "I see that you have already removed the body."

"Yes, Mr. Holmes," the representative of the law responded. "Tide was coming in and I knew it would do no good to have the corpse submerged in seawater." A smile crossed Inspector Mackenzie's boyish features. "Mr. Macaulay has already been conveyed to the mortuary and a postmortem will be conducted. We should have the results by this afternoon. All quite forward-thinking of me, eh, Mr. Holmes?"

"Oh, most forward-thinking, inspector," Holmes acerbically answered pointing with his cane. "However, in doing so you have trod back and forth through the scene enough times to obliterate any traces of a second party's footprints."

"I can assure you, Mr. Holmes," Mackenzie said, "that there were no other footprints. Mr. Macaulay's were the only ones to be seen in the sand. I checked the outline with his boots myself."

"My felicitations, Makenzie," Holmes said. "Might I be allowed to inspect the scene for myself?"

Inspector Makenzie made a broad gesture with his arms. Holmes and I pressed on; Laramie shrinking back perhaps still unnerved by the devilish nature of the area.

"Inspector Mackenzie is one of a new breed," Holmes said as we crossed the beach. His eyes were on the ground, darting this way and that looking for a clue of any kind. "His self-assurance is his greatest weakness as a criminal investigator."

"I think it would be inaccurate to suggest that you were never self-assured, Holmes," I replied.

"Ah, your pawky humor has not deserted you, Watson," Holmes said. "However there is one major difference between Inspector Mackenzie and me. I am Sherlock Holmes. He is not."

I could not help but suppress a guffaw at my friend's quip, and I caught once again a glimpse of his fast-moving brain, waiting for mental stimulation. Though I am sure he would never have admitted it, I knew my friend well enough to know that this – searching for clues at the scene of an impossible murder – brought him much greater fulfillment than his colony of bees ever could.

We approached the large stone, and as we drew nearer to the strange object, I could make out the bizarre symbols which Laramie had mentioned. A series of concentric circles, undulating lines, and curious depictions of things which are beyond my powers as a writer, I could easily see how this odd, ancient form of writing could have unnerved the men so. There was almost nothing – to the layman, at least – which suggested its meaning to us. Could these strange symbols be an auspicious omen, or were they a harbinger of doom?

Holmes cast his eyes over the symbols for an instant only before he had approached the stone and ran a hand over its rough surface. He drew this hand away, and then reached into his pocket, withdrawing his familiar magnifying lens. He peered at the stone once more beneath the lens and murmured to himself all the while.

"Anything?" I said at length.

"It is curious," Holmes muttered more to himself than to me. "Curious indeed."

He then turned on his heel and strode away, his examination seemingly complete.

"Dr. Laramie," Holmes called out to our client who stood quieting conversing with the representative of the law, "you said something about this stone weeping blood. Can you be more specific?"

Laramie drew in a deep breath. "I do not know what I can possibly tell you, Mr. Holmes. I am at a loss. We all are. The stone has been known to weep blood from time to time. Never much, mind you, but blood trickles out from the stone."

"Is it genuine?" Holmes asked.

"I'd like to think that I know blood when I see it," Laramie rebuked. Holmes pressed on:

"And this strange stone," Holmes said, "it is your opinion that it comes from South America?"

"It has all the hallmarks of having come from that corner of the world," Laramie said. "The quality of the stone is similar to other rock deposits found there, and the markings – verified by one of my colleagues – do seem to be Incan. How it arrived here in England is a mystery to me."

No sooner had Holmes processed this staggering assessment than he was turning his attention wholly to

Inspector Mackenzie once more: "You say the body has been taken to the mortuary?"

"Yes, Mr. Holmes. An autopsy was to be scheduled immediately."

"I should have liked to search the body *in situ*, but under the circumstances..." Holmes's voiced trailed off. "You would not be averse to Dr. Watson making an examination of Mr. Macaulay's mortal remains, inspector?"

"Not at all, Mr. Holmes," the cocksure young inspector replied. "I should welcome any opinion that you may have."

"Then it is the morgue that we shall next visit," Holmes declared.

Laramie said that he was going to oversee the site once more and offered us the use of his automobile and driver. Gratefully accepting, we made our way back to where the vehicle was parked on the promontory overlooking the beach. Once seated inside, Holmes instructed the driver to take us to the village police station. As we sat, I heard Holmes sigh satisfactorily and I realized quite suddenly that Sherlock Holmes and I were no longer the young men we once were. I am sure that leaping once more into the fray as he was,

Holmes still fancied himself the energetic investigator, ready to throw himself face-first onto the ground in order to examine the scene for clues. But, to do so now was almost an impossibility. Holmes and I were both pushing sixty years of age. I suddenly felt my age; memories of my many years at Holmes's side suddenly played out before me and I recalled that in my time I had lived twice as much as most men. A dry chuckle escaped my lips.

"You find this all amusing, Watson," Holmes said turning to me.

"Hardly," I remarked. "I was simply reminiscing. This feels like the old days, does it not?"

Holmes laughed. "Indeed, it does. You asked me before we were interrupted by Dr. Laramie if I miss it: being London's only unofficial consulting detective. Our little adventure today seems to suggest that I have nothing to miss. And, but a few years ago I was engaged on another littler matter which resolved itself in the queerest of ways. Really, Watson, one of these days I must tell you about the Lion's Mane. It is a story which, if ever written, I should think that no reader would believe."

"I feel quite similarly about this business," I said. "A stone which weeps blood. It's fantastic. Do you have any idea what caused Macaulay's death?"

"I have my suspicions," Holmes replied. "It is still too early for me to speak them aloud lest I bias not only your judgment but my own. But, if my supposition is correct, then Dr. Laramie may have wished that he had never taken it upon himself to study that strange, weeping stone."

The coroner – a big, bearded man called Mitchell – showed us into the mortuary. It had, thankfully, been some years since I had been surrounded by death, and the unpleasant smell of the morgue was one which assailed my nostrils as soon as we entered that pristine, tiled room.

"Devon Macaulay," Dr. Mitchell said, as he strode into the room, "aged six-and-twenty. By my estimation, he was dead for nearly six hours before he was discovered on the beach this morning."

Approaching the slab on which the body had been laid out, Mitchell withdrew the white shroud which covered Macaulay's mortal remains. Holmes and I glanced down at the body of the young man and I felt a twinge of sadness for a life which was extinguished so soon. I then recoiled in surprise for Dr. Laramie's words had been apt. It looked as if Macaulay had been frightened to death. His eyes, wide in alarm and his mouth agape as if he were still screaming from beyond the grave, are sights I shall never forget.

Holmes knelt close to the body, passing his critical all-seeing eyes over the dead man.

"Are there signs of heart failure?" I asked. "The rictus is indicative of such."

"None that I could detect, Doctor," Mitchell replied. "And by all accounts, Macaulay was a hearty, healthy young man. It would be very unlikely that he had a weak heart."

"Then how do you account for the look of utter terror on his face?"

"I don't know," Mitchell replied. "His body shows no signs of violence at all. Poor man must have *seen* something in his last moments of life though."

Sherlock Holmes indicated with a finger that I should draw closer to the body.

"His left leg, Watson," he said. "Feel it."

I did as I was instructed. "The muscle, it's stiff as a board. Far exceeding rigor mortis," I declared.

"Suggesting what?"

"A powerful poison of some kind," I replied.

"*Poison*?!" Mitchell cried. "Surely not!"

"Surely it is so, Doctor," Holmes retorted sardonically. "It would do you and Inspector Mackenzie good to begin treating Mr. Macaulay's death as a violent one."

No sooner had Holmes made such a declaration than Inspector Mackenzie strode into the room, a prideful grin on his face.

"Speak of the devil and he shall appear," Holmes murmured.

"I could not help but overhear, Mr. Holmes," Mackenzie said. "And it looks as if I have beaten you at your own game. What do you like to say: 'This is a case of murder. Cold, calculating, deliberate murder'? Well, I am happy to announce that I have a suspect in custody at this very moment."

"Bravo, inspector," Holmes blandly rebuked. "And just who is this unfortunate person?"

"Mr. Malcolm Anderson," Mackenzie answered. "Dr. Laramie's fellow researcher and Macaulay's rival for the affections of Laramie's daughter, Rebecca. But the morgue is no place for a conversation like this. Let us decamp to my office and we can talk the thing through there."

A moment later we were in Mackenzie's small corner office, a room overcrowded with papers. I sat across from the boyish inspector who seemed to be engulfed by the large chair in which he sat, while Holmes stood by the open window, pulling contentedly on a newly-lit cigarette.

"It was really quite obvious," Mackenzie was saying, "it merely took a little creative thinking. Mr. Anderson was one of the last people to see Macaulay alive. According to Miss Laramie, Anderson and Macaulay had an argument before Macaulay's death. Obviously, wishing to see the score settled, Anderson followed Macaulay out of the inn, trailed him to the beach, and poisoned him."

"Excellent, inspector," Holmes said turning away from the window. "Excellent work."

A smug looked crossed Inspector Mackenzie's face.

"You have only failed to provide Mr. Anderson with a proper motive, a method of murder, and an explanation as to how he managed to follow Macaulay onto the beach without leaving any footprints in the sand."

Mackenzie's face fell. "Well," he began, "that can all be explained away. Anderson and Macaulay were obviously quarreling about something. Raised tempers lead to the violence between men. He must have had some quantity of poison on his person, and forcing Macaulay to take it, he left the same way he had come, being sure to tread only in Macaulay's own footprints."

Holmes crushed his cigarette into an ashtray. "Your theory answers some of my questions, inspector, but it presents plenty of questions on its own. Frankly, you have fallen into the same habit as my former friends at Scotland Yard of concocting theories before one is in full possession of the facts. You have begun to twist your facts to pin the blame on Mr. Anderson alone. Think of it, inspector: what earthly reason should Mr. Anderson have for keeping a quantity of some deadly poison on his person? And if he had managed to force it upon Mr. Macaulay, why should the dead man have a look of utter terror upon his face, and not pain from the attack?"

Mackenzie considered the detective's words for a moment and then remained silent. Obviously he had no rebuttal.

"Might Dr. Watson and I have a word with Mr. Anderson?" Holmes asked at length.

Mackenzie nodded, clearing his throat as he stood. "He has been detained for further questioning. If you gentleman would follow me this way."

Mackenzie led us out of his office and down a corridor towards what I soon discovered amounted to the constabulary's jail. Passing a uniformed officer, Mackenzie gestured for us to enter the small, cramped, barred room in which sat an unfortunate-looking young man who sat clasping and unclasping his hands, a look of equal parts irritation and dejection writ heavily upon his brow.

"Mr. Malcolm Anderson," Holmes intoned as we stepped into the cell. The young man looked up and nodded. "My name is Sherlock Holmes and this is my friend and colleague, Dr. John Watson. We understand that you are currently being held in connection with the death of Mr. Devon Macaulay. I would like to put a few questions to you."

Anderson's tense shoulders lowered. What a relief it must have been for someone to speak to him so calmly when I am sure that the vainglorious Inspector Mackenzie did little but belittle the young man in an effort to crush his spirit and elicit a confession.

"I didn't kill Devon," Anderson said. "I had an almighty row with him, that I will admit, but I did not kill him."

"This row," Holmes said. "What was it about?"

"Rebecca," Anderson replied after a moment. "Miss Laramie. Both Devon and I were rather keen on her."

"You were rivals for her affections?" I said.

Anderson nodded. "We would both go to the ends of the earth for her, and neither of us was willing to let the other have her. We had sparred over it on a number of occasions in the past, and last night Rebecca – er, Miss Laramie – and I were alone. We were seated, quietly talking in the lounge of the Tiger Inn when Macaulay came in and sat himself down at the table. I tried to get him to go but he wouldn't leave. I lost my head, Mr. Holmes; I started yelling the foulest things at him. I admit it and I regret it."

"What did you do next?"

"Macaulay sat and took it," Anderson said. "He weathered every insult, every name under the sun that I could conjure, and then at last he stood and strode off with his head high." Anderson chuckled in spite of himself. "The blackguard was a bigger man than me, it seemed.

"But that just caused my temper to flare up all the more. I stormed out after him, yelling at him even as he strode away from me. He didn't turn to face me once. Once he had disappeared from my view, I turned to rejoin Miss Laramie but she had gone. I do not blame her."

"These insults," Holmes said, "what did you say? What precisely were your choicest words?"

Again Anderson chuckled; a dry, sardonic laugh totally devoid of mirth. "Honest to god, Mr. Holmes, I don't remember. I lost my head completely. I remember speaking, but the words themselves...they're gone."

"That is most unfortunate," Holmes replied. "But believe me when I tell you that I do believe you. I do not think for one moment that you murdered Mr. Macaulay. I shall do my utmost to clear your name as soon as possible."

"My thanks, Mr. Holmes. I have had some time to think on what I have done and I could not be more ashamed.

Even if you absolve me of this crime, can you take away my own guilt?"

Holmes seemed to be in an even more contemplative mood than usual as we emerged from the station. It was the early afternoon now, the sun slowly beginning to hang lower in the sky. The breeze over the ocean had strengthened and I felt a chill pass up my spine as we stepped outside.

"And our next port-of-call is?" I asked.

"I rather think that we shan't have to leave this very spot," Holmes replied.

I looked in the direction of my friend's gaze and saw a handsome young woman disembark from an automobile. As she approached, Holmes called to her:

"Miss Laramie, I presume?"

"You know me?" the woman asked, tentatively drawing closer to we older strangers.

"The resemblance to your father is a marked one," Holmes replied. "My name is Sherlock Holmes."

"The *detective*?" she countered. A smile crossed Holmes's mouth.

"The same. Quite by chance I was called in to investigate the matter of Mr. Devon Macaulay's unfortunate death. Might my friend and colleague, Dr. Watson, and I have a word with you? It could go a great way towards bringing this matter to a satisfactory conclusion."

"I shall help in any way that I can to clear up Devon's death," the young woman replied.

"Excellent," Holmes said. "Allow us to step just inside for I observed Dr. Watson take some offense to the decided chill in the afternoon air."

We stepped back into the lobby of the police station, Holmes and I doffing our hats as we did so. I elected to take a seat and Miss Laramie followed suit. Only Holmes remained standing, pacing back and forth as he addressed the young lady:

"You were doubtlessly on your way to speak with Mr. Anderson?"

"That is correct, Mr. Holmes. When I last saw Malcolm, he was in quite an unpleasant frame of mind. My father had just informed me that he has been suspected of murdering Devon and duly arrested. That cannot be true, can it?"

"I am quite confident in Mr. Anderson's innocence," Holmes answered. "But it is Mr. Anderson's *unpleasant frame of mind* which I wished to address. The young man has freely admitted that he spoke quite coarsely with Macaulay last night just before his death. What exactly did Mr. Anderson say?"

Faint traces of red rose in Miss Laramie's cheeks. "I should not wish to repeat everything that Malcolm said word-for-word, you understand. However he was insulting Devon's bravery. His confidence. His manhood, Mr. Holmes."

"Was Mr. Macaulay not by nature a confident man?"

"Sadly, no," Miss Laramie said. "Devon was rather weak-willed, I'm afraid. He would frequently dine with my father and me and Devon could barely stomach some of the stories about ancient practices. One evening we discussed Incan sacrificial rituals over drinks and Devon sat, white as a sheet, throughout it all. Malcolm called Devon a child; a child who was wholly terrified of that queer weeping stone.

"Malcolm told Devon that a real man would be able to face that rock. That he could even approach it and stand on it if need be. Malcolm teased him endlessly saying that Devon could never do it. And then Devon stood quite suddenly, wished me good evening, and strode out of the room. Malcolm followed him out and kept yelling at him but I had had quite enough. I went up to my room and refused to speak to anyone for the rest of the night."

Sherlock Holmes considered. "Miss Laramie, you have been of invaluable assistance to me. And if you may permit an old man to speak for another moment: please do not begrudge Mr. Anderson. He feels responsible for Mr. Macaulay's death, and he resents his temper for getting the better of him. Mr. Anderson is quite keen on you. He told me himself. Go to him, Miss Laramie. If my suspicions prove correct, he may look to you for strength in the coming days."

Holmes turned to go but was arrested by the sound of Miss Laramie's voice:

"Is he somehow responsible for this, Mr. Holmes? You said you believe him to be innocent but…"

"We shall know in time, Miss Laramie."

Then without a further word, Holmes had left the room. I caught up to him outside.

"Now what?" I asked.

"We wait," Holmes replied. "I should like to conduct a little experiment but it will be best if we carry it out by moonlight. In the meantime, let us enjoy an early supper. We shall want our strength about us tonight. I predict something of an ordeal is in our future."

We dined at Holmes's that evening; as usual, my friend refused to speak of the case and instead pressed me for details about life in London. For the first time that day I felt as if my reunion with Holmes was going as planned, and it was wonderful to reminiscence about days of old with the man at whose side I had spent so many years. Truth be told, I thought I detected a rueful glint in Holmes's grey eyes as I spoke of London and my occasional run-ins with Inspector Lestrade or Stanley Hopkins of Scotland Yard; acquaintances whose presence on our doorstep was not out of ordinary at all. I spoke too of my practice which now occupied my days when, years ago, I might have accompanied Holmes into some den of criminality in order to bring to book some cunning rogue. How the times had changed.

The sun had completely sunk below the horizon and the moon was ever so slowly taking its place in the sky when we set out. Holmes had equipped himself with a silver-headed walking stick (and had demonstrated its weighted head to me in his gloved hand before we had struck out) and an electric torch. We set out on foot, headed back towards the excavation – the site of Devon Macaulay's death and the weeping stone. Holmes was silent about his intentions as we descended the rocky crag towards the beach and once we had arrived at the abandoned site, I could not help but pull up the collar of my coat as the breeze blew off the ocean and whipped around us. The rhythmic lapping of the ocean on the shoreline seemed miles away as Holmes and I slowly advanced across the sand, the detective's gaze fixed squarely on the strange stone.

We were just short of the weird edifice when Holmes clapped a hand to my shoulder. "Stay back, Watson. For god's sake be careful."

"Of what?" I incredulously responded.

Holmes put a finger to his lips and then carefully stepped towards the stone. He then stopped, lifted the stick high over his head and brought it down upon the stone with a loud *thwack*. I stared at my friend in utter uncomprehending disbelief. Had I been asked on the spot to elucidate Holmes's actions, I could not have done it for the world. And yet he seemed entirely confident in what he did, repeatedly hitting the stone with his stick once more, then again, and again, and again. At last we stepped back and reached out an arm as though protecting me from something.

That was when the weeping stone bore its terrible secrets.

I watched first in fascination then horror as the stone began to weep blood. Slowly, the thick, viscus substance crawled down its side. We watched as blood oozed out of the rock and only seconds later the stone yielded another impossibility. Seemingly from the rock's very bowels, the largest spider I had ever seen in my life crawled into view. The creature was surely no smaller than the dinner plates on which we had just eaten that evening, and to see the thing move slowly across the blood-stained surface of the rock made my skin crawl, and the hairs on the back of my neck stand on end. This monstrous apparition was followed by another and another until at least five hideously large arachnids were scurrying across the surface of the stone. Now I knew why Holmes had insisted on such precautions.

"They are nothing less than monsters, Watson," Holmes murmured. "Creatures from the deepest pit of the South American jungle. Spiders large enough to hunt birds and endowed with poison powerful enough to kill animals three times their size. Poor Devon Macaulay hadn't a chance when he ventured down here last evening."

One of the spiders crawled its way towards us and instinctively I stepped back, fearful that the beast might lunge at us from the rock putting its eight long legs to use. Holmes reached out with his stick and brought the weighted end down upon the creature's thorax. I looked away as stick met animal and the spider quickly died. I felt no remorse whatsoever for its passing.

Holmes repeated the act with the several other spiders which soon crawled towards what remained of their kind. He dispatched all of them and, having done so, I caught a glimpse of my friend reaching a hand into his inner pocket and producing a handkerchief. First he passed the fabric across his brow and then clapped it to his mouth. To have destroyed so many hideous creatures so rapidly was, indeed, a nauseating act.

"They are all dead?" I said.

"We can only hope," Holmes replied. "But let us be on our guard nonetheless. You may not think it prudent, my dear fellow, but I wish to inspect the rock more closely."

I followed Holmes close behind as we cautiously drew nearer the stone. Holmes switched on the torch and rounded the back of the rock; a side of the strange monolith we had not yet seen. He cast the beam of light around the rock and then kneeling, Holmes let out an exclamation of satisfaction and gestured for me to join him on the sand below. As I did so, I could plainly see what appeared to be a hollow crevice which extended up into the depths of the strange stone.

"Just as I suspected from the fore," Holmes said. "The rock is hollow. While we were so concerned with the odd markings on the opposite side, we never seemed to pay any heed to any other part of the stone. It is from here that those hideous creatures sprang. But let us be away from here, Watson. We do not know how many more reside within still and I do not wish to know the answer."

Forty-five minutes later we were ensconced in the warm environs of Holmes's parlor once more. We nursed glasses of brandy and the familiar figures of Dr. Laramie, his daughter, and Inspector Mackenzie sat opposite us on Holmes's settee.

"From the beginning," Holmes was saying as he settled in his seat, "my curiosity was aroused by the blood which was purported to weep from the stone. I knew from that point on that the stone must not be what it seemed. The blood must come from somewhere within so I knew that the stone was, at least partially, hollow. My supposition was confirmed when I noted that the stone had barely made any impression in the sand. A rock that size would surely have showed signs from where it fell upon the beach if it had been displaced from the cliff face as has been suggested during a collapse. Since there were none, I knew that the rock could not have been heavy as it was and had not been lodged in the side of the cliff. The strange, weeping stone was indeed from South America; its lightness making it buoyant enough to have floated all this way.

"Figuring, then, that the rock was hollow led me to wonder what else could be recessed within. My mind raced with possibilities but it did not take me long to settle on some kind of venomous creature which could have easily done the unfortunate Devon Macaulay to death. The horrified expression on his face suggested that whatever creature it was is a particularly nasty one so I postulated spiders. That could be my own bias coming out, however. All of these suspicions were confirmed when I examined Macaulay's body and discovered that his limbs had gone entirely stiff; evidence of some powerful poison in his bloodstream. Additionally, I perceived several small pricks just above Macaulay's ankle where he was bitten by the spiders' poisonous fangs. Dr. Mitchell would certainly never have noticed it or given it much heed, but I was looking for it. What is more, this accounts for the mysterious illnesses of some of the men. Without even knowing it, they disturbed the resting place of the spiders as they worked. One single spider bite may not have been enough to kill a man but merely to put him down for a few days.

"The spiders, too, explain away what you perceived to be blood weeping from the stone, Dr. Laramie. You told me that you had not studied it, and the viscous substance – some byproduct of the creatures within, no doubt, surely looked – to the untrained eye, at least – like blood. You would surely be the first to confess, Doctor, that you are no entomologist. To you, the substance was blood, and you had little reason to suspect anything else.

"The circumstances, then, of Devon Macaulay's death were of the most unfortunate kind. Goaded on by Mr. Anderson's taunts last evening, Macaulay left with the intent of facing his fear and going down to the rock. I am sure that this was done in some bid to win your affections, Miss Laramie. Macaulay did just as Anderson had told him: to face the rock and – if need be – to stand on it. Macaulay approached the rock alone, clambered up onto it, and waited. The act of doing so, however, disturbed the spiders resting just inches below his feet beneath the porous membrane of the rock's outer surface. So disturbing them, they crawled out to investigate. Macaulay was caught unawares, and surely scared half to death. He managed to jump down from the rock but not before he was stuck by several of the spiders and fell dead upon the spot; the poison killing him almost instantaneously."

Holmes paused to take a sip of his drink.

"As I said earlier, Miss Laramie, we would soon see whether Mr. Anderson could be implicated in Mr. Macaulay's death. I argue that he remains guiltless. Macaulay's death was entirely an accident. He had no reason to suspect that the weeping stone harbored a secret so strange…or so deadly."

"Malcolm shall never forgive himself," Miss Laramie murmured.

"In time he must," Holmes said. "I urge you to help him as best you can."

A rueful smile played upon Miss Laramie's lips.

"And as for you, Dr. Laramie," Holmes continued, "I suggest that you take even further precautions should you wish to examine the mysterious stone further. It may not yet have given up all its secrets. Were I in your place, Doctor, I should return the stone to the ocean where it once was."

"But I cannot," Laramie cried. "It is an archaeological discovery unparalleled in this century. The stone has only begun to tell us about our ancient world. Surely if we study it further, a whole host of questions can finally be answered."

"Perhaps," Holmes said, "those questions deserve to go unanswered."

I saw Laramie suppress a groan as the telephone rang in the next room. Holmes rose and excused himself, instructing me to show our guests out, insisting that the inspector free Anderson at once.

I returned to the room as Holmes hung up the phone. Across his habitually cruel mouth, he wore a wry smile. "That was my brother on the phone," he announced settling into his seat. "He has been contacted by the Home Secretary. Storm clouds are gathering over Europe, Watson, and Mycroft wishes for me to play a small part in preventing it. He has asked me to come up to London on the first train tomorrow. I shouldn't wish to end our weekend prematurely, so would you care to accompany me?"

As I sat across from Holmes, I suddenly had the impression that time was ticking backwards. We were no longer in the twentieth century; two men entering our dotage regarding each other from our seats in a parlor on the Sussex Downs. Once more it was 1895. Holmes and I were young again, and we were back in 221b Baker Street. A fire crackled in the grate, taking the chill out of the damp air. A fog swirled outside the window. A hansom cab rattled over the ancient cobbles, and somewhere in the distance the bells of Big Ben chimed the hour. The tableau was one which I had experienced so many times in my life: a comfortable, familiar scene which was forever etched in my memory. And it was playing out again now.

"I should happy to, Holmes," I replied. "I would not miss it for the world."

Sherlock Holmes – young or old, it mattered not – jumped up from his seat. Reaching for his Inverness and deerstalker, he exclaimed: "Then come along, my dear Watson. *The game is afoot!*"

Death in the House of the
Black Madonna

Originally Published in The MX Book of New Sherlock
Holmes Stories: Part XVIII

I

"Ah, Sherlock, Dr. Watson," said Mycroft Holmes without rising from his overstuffed leather chair, "it does me good to see two such familiar faces after so long a time."

It had been several years – seemingly several lifetimes – since I had stood in the Stranger's Room, the only room in which speaking was permitted within the austerity of the Diogenes Club, and it felt nearly as long since I had clapped eyes upon my old friend, Mr. Sherlock Holmes. On that particular day in the early summer of 1919, I felt as if I were separated by oceans of time from the man I once was at Holmes' side; friend and colleague to the world's first unofficial consulting detective. At the dawn of the Great War, I had assisted Holmes in some official state business, but in the intervening years, we drifted apart. I heard tell from Holmes' occasional correspondences that he had been employed once more by his brother and the British Secret Service to carry out matters of state, and I do confess that a part of me felt jealous that my friend was still continually challenging himself just as he was so many years earlier. For my part I did all that I could to aide in the war effort and resumed my practice with a zealous attitude that was unrivaled since my earliest days as a practicing medico. It was stimulating work, but each time I received a letter from Holmes – the man positively detested the modern convenience of the telephone – I yearned to be at his side once again.

So, when I received an urgent telegram from him that morning informing me of his presence in London and requesting me to meet him at noon precisely in the Stranger's Room of the Diogenes Club, I could not have been more surprised or more thrilled.

As my eyes fell upon Sherlock Holmes once more, I was amazed to see that he had changed little since last we had met. He was just as tall and lean as ever, though age had begun to show upon his pointed, aquiline features, and his temples had gone the way of grey. He leaned upon a silver-handled walking stick, and even at a glance I could see that there was a stiffness to his legs which spoke of some recently sustained injury which, even for a man as healthy as Holmes, was not the kind of damage that could be easily sustained by a man firmly in his sixties. His grey eyes twinkled as I drew into the room which was promptly closed behind me by the porter who had shown me in, and I barely had a chance to greet him before Mycroft Holmes was addressing the both of us and waving us into the two empty chairs that were facing him with his large hands.

"I must admit, Sherlock," Mycroft was continuing, "that there was some reticence upon my part when you suggested to me this morning that you should like to involve Dr. Watson in this affair. However, seeing as the man does have a habit of bringing the best out of you, I acquiesced to your wishes."

I had never known Mycroft to speak so highly of me and I blushed in spite of myself.

"You shall want your wits about you, brother mine," Mycroft continued, "as this case is a matter of international security."

"You have been characteristically taciturn about the details of this case, Mycroft," Holmes said, as he eased into his own chair, and stiffly crossed one leg over the other. Then settling back in his seat, he withdrew his silver cigarette case from the breast pocket of his coat, coaxed a cylinder from amongst its brethren, and lighted it. "However, you promise much and I expect much for having traveled so far from my bees at so volatile a time for the colony."

Mycroft scoffed. "You shall find this business more fruitful to your constitution, Sherlock, than your bees and your honey ever could be. I do know how you crave mental exercise."

Holmes blew a ring of smoke about his gaunt head. "Then, please," he said, "do not hesitate any longer in telling to us the details in full."

Mycroft shifted his girth in his chair. "It could hardly have escaped your attention, gentleman, that precisely one year ago, the kingdoms of Bohemia and Moravia united into one country, Czechoslovakia. This peaceful transition of power was admired the world over, particularly as it came so close on the heels of the Great War. When that conflict came to an end and word began to spread through the seats of power in Europe that such a unification was imminent, His Majesty's Government sent an agent, a reliable man called Fitzroy, to be our own eyes and ears on the ground. He reported to Prague in April of last year and oversaw the official process from afar. We received bi-weekly reports from Fitzroy, oftentimes encoded should they be inadvertently intercepted in transmission from the continent, and in each report he spoke of what progress was being made within the country.

"Six weeks ago, however, the nature of Fitzroy's reports began to change. He alluded to a scheme of some variety, however details were sparse and he dared not reveal too much, even in the form of a coded message, should it fall into the wrong hands. We received two messages of this nature from Fitzroy before all communication stopped. We have not heard from Fitzroy at all since his last communication which confirmed that something was afoot in the city of Prague. We immediately dispatched another man to the continent in search of Fitzroy, but his efforts yielded nothing. When he returned with only one piece of information, it was decided that we should bring in someone else to oversee the location of our man. I suggested you, Sherlock."

Mycroft Holmes sat back in his seat as Holmes smoked his cigarette in silence. I stared from one brother to the other waiting for this informal standoff to end. It did when the younger Holmes said:

"So you wish me to go to Prague?"

"Yes. Your mission is to locate Fitzroy and – if possible – to elicit from him the details of this plot onto which he has stumbled."

Holmes crushed the cigarette into an ashtray and hoisted himself from his seat. "I daresay that you could have selected a better man for this job, Mycroft. This espionage work is hardly the business of an old man like me. And, you can hardly forget what happened in Constantinople." Holmes gestured with his cane at his leg. The injury was sustained during some mission, then.

"I can think of no better man than you, Sherlock." Mycroft then added as an afterthought, "And of course you too, Dr. Watson."

I bowed my head resolutely.

"This matter should hardly require of you the same physical prowess as the Turkish Job," Mycroft said, as he pulled himself out of his chair. "Fitzroy and our second man, Jones, are two of our best operatives and combined they do not have the cognitive abilities to adequately investigate this business. You, alone, Sherlock, can handle this matter."

I saw Holmes stare at a point in the floor and consider. This business was so far afield from the little matters which were presented to us in our Baker Street rooms years ago. This was a matter of international consequence, and despite Holmes' considerable efforts in the past, I could tell that he felt daunted by the task before him. Then, miraculously, the ghost of a smile crept across Holmes' thin lips and he turned his gaze to me.

"I shall be happy to handle this investigation for you, Mycroft, provided Dr. Watson is keen to accompany me. Even after all these years I should be lost without my Boswell."

I felt a sudden surge of joy rush through my breast and I all but jumped out of my chair. "I should like nothing more, Holmes!" I cried.

"Splendid," the detective replied. Then, rounding on his brother with newfound alertness and energy, he said: "I shall, of course, require a few hours prep time before Dr. Watson and I make accommodations to catch the boat train. If my memory of the time tables is still exact then we should have no difficulty in catching the 3.06."

"That would be the 3.08, brother mine," Mycroft countered with a wry grin.

"But of course," Holmes retorted, acquiescing to his intellectual superior. "I did myself the service of packing a few spare clothes before I departed Sussex but I should expect that the good Doctor will need an opportunity to pack a spare shirt and pair of trousers for the continent."

"I should welcome the opportunity," I replied.

"And do be a good fellow and slip your old service revolver between yours things," Holmes added. "That is, provided you still have the thing about."

I nodded in the affirmative.

"Excellent!" Holmes exclaimed. "I shall require one more crucial piece of information from you, Mycroft: You say that this second man, Jones, discovered something while he was in Prague searching for Fitzroy. What did this man discover?"

"An all-important but ultimately fruitless lead, I am afraid," Mycroft said. "According to Jones, Fitzroy is still alive. Jones' contacts in the city have heard word that he is still alive but in hiding. Fitzroy has done a good enough job in going to ground that even Jones could not locate him."

"These contacts of Jones'," Holmes said, "could you supply me with their names as well?"

"I shall examine his report and send you their names this afternoon."

"And a photograph of Fitzroy shall be of great assistance."

"Of course," Mycroft replied.

Holmes beamed. "Then I do not think we should waste another moment here," he declared. Turning to me, he said, "Come, Watson. Once more the game is afoot!"

II

We did part ways after we had left the Diogenes Club, rushing out into the teeming streets of Whitehall. I called out for a passing cab while Holmes rushed off down the street, already in the midst of setting some plan into action. I returned home and hurriedly packed a bag, making sure that I tucked my old revolver amongst my things as Holmes requested. I then traveled by automobile once more and arrived at Victoria Station just in time to meet Holmes for the 3.08 train to Dover.

Situated within a train carriage opposite from my friend melted away the years and for a brief instant I felt as if we were back on opposite sides of the hearth in Baker Street. Holmes regaled me with tales of his recent exploits, though in his habitual tight-lipped fashion, he never indulged on the details and often left me yearning to know more. The fabled mission to Constantinople, for instance, he never once mentioned. He was also kind enough to press me for information of my life since last we had met and I was happy to share my successes as a practicing physician. A light came into Holmes's eyes as we sat in the undulating carriage and watched the countryside pass us by.

"It does me good to see you again, old man," he said.

"And it does me good to see you too, Holmes," I replied with a great grin. "This is just like old times."

"We may be older and greyer, but indeed, this is like old times," Holmes replied bemusedly.

"And if this is indeed like old times," I continued, "then I ought to know you well enough to know that you have already set into motion some scheme. I saw you hurry out of the Diogenes like a man possessed. What is to be our plan of action?"

Holmes grinned and leaned forward conspiratorially. "I should think it best, my dear fellow," he began, "that we should maintain a discreet profile once we have arrived in

Prague. I fear that we tread in dark waters and making our presence known would be a mistake of a cataclysmic kind."

I agreed with my friend, though his gloomy words unnerved me.

"In spite of this – or perhaps as a result of it – I have been forced to make contact with some of Prague's more shadowy operatives, a task I set into motion this afternoon. I secured the name of one of Jones' contacts in Prague, a man called Palan, who has agreed to meet us as soon as we arrive. It is through Palan that I hope that we shall find our way to Fitzroy."

"Was Mycroft able to supply you with a photograph of the man?"

Holmes nodded and withdrew a folded picture from his inner pocket; a portrait of a youngish, handsome man with dark hair and a prominent jaw. I studied his features for a moment – enough I felt confident that I could recognize the fellow on sight – and then returned it to Holmes.

"We have a long journey ahead of us, Watson," Holmes said as he leaned his head back against the plush seat. "I recommend getting some sleep now. I think that we shall need all of our wits about us very soon."

Yet it felt as if it took ages for us to eventually reach the city of Prague. Our connecting train in France crawled through Central Europe, climbing through mountains and forging through deep valleys that for many hours I felt as if I were in a state of total disorientation; unsure of what way was what. Holmes was silent for much of our journey, and I wondered if – as we wound our way through the land I should forever think of as Bohemia – he cast his mind back to the regal figure of that land who stood within our very Baker Street sitting room so many years ago and hired Holmes for a job; a job which would bring him into direct contact with *the* woman, Irene Adler. Of course, Holmes' face was a mask as he cast his eyes out of the train compartment window and I knew full well that I would never know what he was thinking.

I heaved a great sigh of relief, then, when our train finally reached Prague. Night had fallen over the city and after we collected our bags and found an automobile that was willing to convey us to our hotel. I was thoroughly exhausted. Once instituted within the confines of my room, I sat upon the edge of my bed and let out a deep sigh of total fatigue. Sherlock Holmes, however, was totally unmoved by the long journey and as he stood in the doorway to my room, a look of impatience upon his face, I knew that I had to muster all of my energy to follow him once more. I slipped my revolver into my inner pocket and followed him out into the night.

Our small but comfortable lodgings were situated in Old Town Square, a remarkable open-air square that was surrounded on two sides by churches and on the other the Old Town Hall, a great stone edifice that had been standing for nearly six-hundred years. As we took off that night, Holmes traversing a path through the square as though he knew the place like the back of his hand. The city was eerily quiet as we made our way through its narrow streets and across its ancient cobblestones. Somewhere in the distance, tolling the hour from one of the city's many church steeples, I heard bells signaling the passing of one o'clock in the morning. I felt drained of life as Holmes pulled me down another side street, and I very nearly let out a thankful breath when he whispered that our port of call was at the end of the street.

I saw it at once; a sign for a pub which hung beneath a single streetlamp affixed to the side of a stone building. The sign read something in Czech that I could not divine, but Holmes knew full well that this was the place we needed to be. Approaching the door to the establishment, I thought it very unlikely that anyone should answer Holmes' knock, but much to my surprise, the door swung open from within and we were confronted by a tall, skeletal-looking man with a countenance that spoke of many years' hard labor. Holmes addressed the man briefly in Czech to which he bowed his head and then gestured for us to draw in further. The door closed behind us, I found myself standing in a low, dingy room illuminated only by a few guttering candle flames that stood upon tabletops. The pub was empty save for a few disreputable-looking figures hunched in the shadows. There sat one man, however, at one of the tables, his face lit by the glow of the little candle flame and it was to this man that the stranger at the door gestured.

Holmes approached the man and I tentatively followed. As we drew nearer I could make out the man's features. He was tall and lean with an athletic build, and an ovular head which sat atop his strong neck and shoulders. He was almost completely bald, but his face was covered in prematurely-greying whiskers, and I could tell – even in the low light – that there was a twinkle in the man's humorless eyes.

"Mr. Lukáš Palan," Holmes said inquiringly, yet I believe he already knew the answer.

The man nodded his head in the affirmative and wordlessly gestured for us to sit as he returned to his own chair. He then reached for the glass at his elbow and downed a swig of the heady brew within.

"You were most vague in your correspondence, Mr. Holmes," Palan said in his heavily-accented voice.

"I think the same could be said of you, Mr. Palan," Holmes retorted. "Yet I know that if there is any man in this city who can help me locate our man, Fitzroy, it is you. You should be pleased to know that your name is not an unfamiliar one in London."

Palan arched an eyebrow. "That is most distressing, sir," he answered. "I have done my utmost to keep a low profile."

"The London criminal fraternity is like one great spiders web interlaced with another," Holmes began, overlapping his long bony fingers as he spoke. "Word spreads from one thread of one web to a thread of another and so on and so on. However, these words are spoken in voices no louder than whispers, Mr. Palan. Your work is still secret to most."

"Most men are not Sherlock Holmes," Palan retorted. "Yours is a name which we know all too well in this country."

"This is why I must insist upon your absolute discretion, Palan. It has become apparent that our man, Fitzroy, was onto something while here in Prague. Should it be a plot of some kind, we cannot allow its perpetrators to know that we are onto them at all."

Palan nodded understandingly and took any drink from his glass. "Well then," he said, "how can I be of assistance to you?"

"First of all," Holmes said, "tell us what you told our man, Jones. He was your contact. We learned from Jones that Fitzroy is still alive and in this city. How did he come across such information?"

Palan considered. "The criminal network of London may be like a great web, Mr. Holmes," he began, "but here in Prague, we are a tighter-knit community (for the lack of a better word). It is unlikely that if some crime is carried out that someone else would not have heard word of it being perpetrated. This includes, surprisingly enough, murder. It was therefore no mean feat to ascertain whether there had been word of any murders perpetrated recently and, if that was the case, who the dead man was. I learned quite easily for Mr. Jones that no dead man matching Mr. Fitzroy's description had turned up anywhere."

"But what if his appearance was altered to conceal his identity?" I asked.

"Such mysterious deaths of that kind had not been reported by anyone in the criminal classes," Palan answered.

"What is more, Watson," Holmes continued, "Fitzroy was traveling virtually incognito. He would have been a total stranger in this city. No one would have known him and to conceal the identity of a complete stranger does seem rather superfluous."

Holmes returned his attention to Palan. "If you are quite certain that Fitzroy is still alive, where would you suggest looking for him?"

"Prague is an ancient city, Mr. Holmes. There are plenty of places in it that one might disappear should they wish."

Holmes considered. "How much manpower have you got? Can you scout the city for Palan provided I supply you with a description?"

"Our numbers are not strong, Mr. Holmes, but they are not feeble. My eyes and ears on the streets can certainly make an effort at finding Fitzroy."

Holmes smiled. Then, the ghost of a grin was gone from his face as he added: "Tell me, Mr. Palan, no matter how trivial it may seem: has there been anything *unusual* going on in this city of late?"

"*Unusual?*" Palan said, sitting bolt-upright in his seat. "Whatever do you mean?"

"I mean precisely what I say," Holmes retorted coldly. "What has been occurring in this city that is beyond your explanation? I note your obvious concern now, but I perceived that something was amiss from the moment I entered this room. Your man at the door is clearly concealing a stiletto blade within his coat – the uncomfortable position of his arm directly above the handle is a dead giveaway – and I think such precautions are unneeded after one in the morning in this secluded pub…even for a man of such a dubious reputation as yourself."

Palan drew in a deep breath. He also chuckled as he spoke next: "Have you heard of The Golem, Mr. Holmes?"

In the darkness of that pub and at the sudden fear which clouded Lukáš Palan's eyes, I felt a chill pass up and down my spine.

"The legend is not unfamiliar to me," Holmes replied, "though I can hardly claim to have an exact knowledge of it."

"Shall I tell it to you, then?"

Holmes let out a sigh of contempt. Never one for stories, I knew full well that hearing the tale of the Golem would not benefit Holmes in any way. However, Palan added: "I can assure you, sir that it is of vital importance to you to know it."

With a wave of his hand, Holmes sat back in his seat and Palan began again.

"There are hundreds of tales of the Golem throughout the world, Mr. Holmes," Palan said, "however it is in Prague that perhaps the most famous tale is said to have taken place. The Golem has become a fixture of this ancient city's legacy. We all know the basics of the story. But, what if it was not just a story? To put it simply, Mr. Holmes, in the sixteenth century Rabbi Loew is said to have created the Golem – a monolithic

creature born from clay from the banks of the Vltava River –
to protect the residents of the city's Jewish Quarter from
pogroms. The creature was brought to life but soon Loew lost
control of his creation and it became more and more powerful.
The thing escaped its confines and went on a rampage through
the city. According to legend, Loew caught up to the Golem
and incapacitated it. Some say that he pulled the *shem* from
the Golem's mouth and incapacitated the creature, while
others suggest that with his staff Rabbi Loew struck from the
Golem's brow one of the carved Hebrew letters which had
brought the thing to life and, in doing so, the Golem crumbled
before his eyes. However, once it had been destroyed, the
Golem (or what was left of it) was placed in an attic room of
the Old New Synagogue should its services ever be needed
again.

"There are many in this city that believe that that day
has come."

Holmes leaned forward in his chair. "I think you had
better explain yourself, Palan."

"For some time now," Palan continued, "there are
have been sightings of a creature that could only be the Golem.
At first these sightings were reported only by children and not

taken very seriously, but there have been more and more people who have said that they have seen something; a beast in the shape of a man but larger than any mortal man could ever be. He keeps to the shadows and his features are caught only in fleeting glimpses, but that is enough to convince many in Prague that the Golem has returned. Whether he is a good omen to mark our independence or a harbinger of doom we do not know."

Holmes considered for a moment. "None of your contacts have anything to say about this Golem?"

"Nothing at all," Palan answered. "I should have thought that I would know such a character, but his shadowy nature concerns me."

"You don't believe that this thing is really the Golem, do you?" I asked incredulously.

"I do not know, Dr. Watson," Lukáš Palan answered. "I wish that I could be more firm in my beliefs. But I simply cannot be sure."

We left Palan, I with trepidation and uneasiness coursing through my body as we traversed the empty streets of the city once more. My eyes were darting into every darkened doorway, down every alleyway looking for long, looming shadows. I could tell that Holmes was reserving his quiet judgment and at length I could only say to him:

"Were you not at all intrigued by the tale that Palan had to tell?"

"It is an interesting bit of local trivia," Holmes rebuked, "though I doubt that it has much bearing on our present situation."

"But how can you explain it?" I asked.

Holmes shrugged his shoulders. "I shall not explain it away until I need to do so," he said. "At present, these sightings of the Golem have little to do with the disappearance of Fitzroy, and I fear that our visit did little to supply me with direction. We are no closer to finding him, I'm afraid."

We returned to our hotel in silence after that and Holmes shut himself away in his room. I slept fitfully that night, tossing and turning on an uncomfortable bed, my dreams filled with visions of *things* beyond human comprehension. It was not long before I abandoned all hope of sleep and sat up waiting for the dawn.

I was taking breakfast, wearily pouring a cup of coffee, when Holmes swept into the room. He took a seat and happily poured himself a cup.

"Your mood is definitely improved," I said as I applied some jam to a slice of bread.

"I underestimated Palan," Holmes replied. He produced a folded sheet of paper and tossed it across the table to me. I opened it and read the hastily-scrawled message thereon:

We have located Fitzroy – L.P.

"That correspondence was slipped under my door only a few hours after we returned," Holmes said. "Not only did I underestimate Palan and his men's ability to locate Fitzroy, but I underestimated his ability to find our own lodgings."

"Well this is wonderful news," I said. "What do we do now?"

No sooner had I asked then there came a knock on the door. Holmes stood to answer it and we found an enthusiastic Lukáš Palan standing on the other side.

"We have no time to lose, Mr. Holmes," he cried. "One of my men is on his way to intercept Fitzroy now. When he found out that we had located him he made immediate plans to flee Prague. If you do not want to lose him, we must act quickly."

Holmes eagerly grabbed for his hat and stick as I threw down my piece of bread and rushed after the two men.

"He was under our nose the entire time," Palan said, as we walked side by side through Old Town Square once more. I was doing my utmost not to be distracted by the beautiful ancient architecture in the daytime which in the early hours of the morning had loomed ominously above us. Now, the city took on a much more beautiful aspect and I drank in the pastel-colored buildings and centuries-worth of architectural styles standing side-by-side. "We located him in a house just off of Old Town Square, and he should be coming through here any moment."

No sooner had Palan spoken than I could sight of a familiar-looking man across the square. He was tall and dignified in appearance, his dark hair and prominent handsome jaw conjuring up images of the photograph Holmes had shown me on the train in my head. Even from a distance, he knew at once that we were looking directly at him and, locking eyes with our small party, I saw his eyes go wide with alarm and then, shockingly, he turned and bolted away from us.

"Quickly," Holmes hissed, "we don't want to lose him!"

The detective broke away from our group, charging after Fitzroy across Old Town Square. One would never have suspected that Holmes was as old as he was or that he had sustained an injury of any kind watching him run as he did. I had always reckoned Holmes a man fleet of foot, but I doubt if I had ever seen a man run faster than my friend did that day. So startled were both Palan and I both Holmes' sudden change that we were left momentarily stunned before movement took over our own legs and he ran after.

Fitzroy had the advantage of youth and he was quite a ways ahead of Holmes, but I still was able to see him through the small crowd of people who had gathered in the square that morning. Fitzroy ducked down a side street in an effort to evade Holmes, but the detective kept his eyes locked on our quarry. As I followed, I felt my legs begin to give way under me and my lungs burning, but I had to power on. If Holmes could keep up the chase, I told myself, then I certainly could do so too. Palan ran alongside of me, his face a quizzical mask. In the midst of our run he turned to me and cried out:

"I haven't any idea where the man could be going!"

We kept running until we saw Holmes come to a stop ahead of us, bent over double catching his breath. We stopped and I did much the same, drawing deep gasps of air into my lungs that felt as if they were on fire.

"I'm afraid that I lost him," Holmes said through gritted teeth. He looked to Palan for his knowledge of the city.

Our informant's eyes full upon the building before which we stood. It was a three-story building that did not match our surroundings at all; a strange, Cubist monstrosity with great bay windows looking out over the cobblestone street. On the corner, where a stone edifice once stood, was the figure of a woman clinging to the wall.

"The House of the Black Madonna," Palan said. "This is the only place that Fitzroy could have sought refuge. It is a department store," Palan said, "but where better to hide than in plain sight?"

"Then we are doing ourselves a disservice by remaining out here," Holmes said, pushing past us and striding into the shop.

At first I believed the building to be empty save for a shopkeeper who was milling around the showroom. He addressed us in Czech, but Holmes brushed the man off, his eyes darting around the premises. And then his gaze fell upon an open door leading further into the shop. Rushing forward, he disappeared into a separate room. I followed and stopped suddenly when I saw what lay within: Sprawled on the floor of the room near the opening to a passageway disappearing out into the street once more, in a horrible, twisted heap was all that remained of our man Fitzroy.

III

Of course the proper authorities were contacted immediately and we soon found ourselves in the curious position of having to communicate with the Czech police. Palan, our guide and translator, had disappeared upon discovery of the body for fear that his face, a familiar countenance to the police, might implicate him in this affair. Therefore, Holmes and I had a devil of time trying to explain ourselves without giving ourselves up entirely. Luckily, in time, a tall, stout official pushed his way through the assembled crowd of onlookers that had gathered outside the House of the Black Madonna.

He was clothed in a tweed suit and homburg with wire-framed glasses on his round face, and jutting from the corner of his thin-lipped mouth was the stump of a pipe. I watched several of the officers with whom we had been attempting to converse address this man and then he turned his attention to us and addressed us in heavily-accented English:

"Mr. Sherlock Holmes," he said to my friend, "your name is a familiar one. And if you are Holmes," he said then turning to me, "then you must be Dr. Watson. It is an honor to have two such personages in my city, but how unfortunate that you should be present at the scene of a murder. That is your line of work, though, is it not, Mr. Holmes?"

"At one time," Holmes said airily. "I am now very much retired and was simply here on holiday with Dr. Watson."

A grin crossed the man's face as though he did not believe us in the slightest. "I have forgotten to properly introduce myself," he said with a courtly bow, "I am Inspector Jan Horák of the Prague police."

"It is a pleasure to meet you, Inspector," Holmes replied.

The mischievous grin did not leave the Inspector's face. "You must forgive me, Mr. Holmes," he said, "it is certainly a once in a lifetime opportunity to work a case alongside a detective as esteemed as you. If you were investigating this matter – hypothetically, of course – what would your first thoughts be?"

Holmes considered, feigning ignorance. "I should make a thorough examination of the body," he said. "Luckily, it seems as though you and your men have left it *in situ*. I must congratulate you. My friends at Scotland Yard many moons ago were not so thorough."

"Would you be interested in making such an examination?" Inspector Horák said. He was tempting my friend as though he were the serpent in the Garden of Eden.

"I should leave such examinations to Dr. Watson," Holmes replied. The Inspector leveled his gaze at me and arched an eyebrow.

"If I may be of any help," I said, "I should be happy to examine the body."

"Excellent," the Inspector replied. He gestured for us to follow him back into the building.

Indeed, the police had taken the proper precautions of leaving everything intact and as we returned to the room in which Fitzroy had been murdered, I realized for the first time that this was the first opportunity I had had to truly oversee the body. I knelt down over the corpse and made a cursory investigation before I stood again.

"The poor fellow has taken a pretty bad beating," I said. "I shouldn't be surprised if nearly every bone in his body was broken, but it was his neck which did the poor man in."

"*Every bone broken?*" the Inspector echoed.

"Yes," I replied. "It was quite a strong hand that did this nasty thing."

"An inhuman hand?" I heard Holmes mutter. Both the Inspector and I turned surprised gazes towards him. "I have heard recently, Inspector, that there has been a spate of sightings of the mythical Golem in your city. I cannot but think that the two cases are related."

"You are not seriously suggesting that the Golem is responsible for this?" the Inspector said incredulously. "I believed you were a rational man!"

"It was a theory and little more," Holmes said with a dismissive wave of the hand. "My apologies that I could not be more helpful to you, Inspector. And I am afraid that Dr. Watson and I must keep and important appointment."

So saying, Holmes took a hold of my arm and whisked me out of the building.

"What is going on, Holmes?" I asked once we had walked far enough away from the crowd and the penetrating glares of the police officers.

"I fear that I spoke too hastily when I dismissed any connection between the Golem and the disappearance of Fitzroy. Now that the man has been murdered – no doubt to prevent him from telling to us the particulars of the plot he stumbled upon – I can see that the two incidents are not unrelated at all."

"Tell me, Holmes, why did Fitzroy run from us in the first place?"

"No doubt he thought we were part of the plot. Put yourself in his place: you are roused early this morning by Palan's men. You do not know them – it was Jones who made contact with them after all – and fearing that your location has been compromised you leave immediately. And then you see three strangers across the square that run after you. Surely in his last moments of life, Fitzroy was convinced that we were not there to lend him a hand, but to kill him. Unfortunately, someone else did just that.

"However, Fitzroy's last actions do tell us something important: if he was not even aware of all the players in this plot, then it is one of a large scope. That is suggestive in itself."

I saw the familiar contemplative look cross Holmes' face as his mind was transported elsewhere as we walked.

"What do you intend to do now?" I asked at length.

"Going through Fitzroy's things will be most instructive," Holmes said, "and we had best do that before the police find out just who he was. We need not run into the scrutinizing Inspector Horák again."

We returned to our hotel where Holmes spent some time in contacting Lukáš Palan. When we had finally discovered the location of Fitzroy's hideaway – only a short distance away from where we had been staying – we hurried off at once. Holmes gained ingress by convincing a man stepping out of the building that he was a relative of the newest tenant in the building and we were admitted without question. We stealthily ascended a cramped, narrow staircase to the first floor of the building, making sure that there were no police officials that had found their way to Fitzroy's before we did. From his coat, Holmes produced his lock-picking kit and went to work on the door which he opened in only a matter of minutes. Stepping inside, we were met with an overwhelming sight.

The cramped flat that Fitzroy had called home was overstuffed with papers; stacks of pages stood upon every flat surface and other sheets lay scattered across the floor, the window seat, and on bookshelves which were overcrowded with aged tomes. Stacks of books challenged the papers for dominance of the space, and I suddenly felt lost amidst all of the paper to be found on the other side of that door. Holmes was undaunted as ever, and stepped further into the room, his head swiveling about like a great predatory bird's. He ducked into the adjoining room and I followed, happy to find that it was Fitzroy's bed chamber and in quite another state altogether. This room was tidy; the man's bed made and his clothes neatly stacked atop his traveling trunk. Holmes stood in the doorway of this room and tapped his lips in consideration.

"It strikes me as odd, wouldn't you concur, my dear Watson?"

"What strikes you odd?" I asked.

"These rooms," Holmes said with a broad gesture. "The outer room is a disaster, brimming over with books and papers while Fitzroy's own room is perfectly-kept. It strikes me as incongruous and suggestive."

"Suggestive of what?"

"Deception," Holmes replied. "Think, Watson: Fitzroy knew full well that he had been found out. He was hiding for good reason, and knew that should his location be compromised that the perpetrators of this mysterious plot would go searching through his things. Would they not be turned off by a room which looked as if it had already been ransacked? Would their search for answers not be greatly inhibited if they could not find a thing to begin with?"

"So Fitzroy kept the room purposefully cluttered?"

"Precisely," Holmes replied, "and I would wager anything that that means the answers we seek are to be found in that room."

Holmes paced back into the room, his eyes darting around him. He suddenly let out an exclamation. "Oh, what a clever, clever man he was, Watson! Mycroft told us that Fitzroy sent all of his communications back to London in code. The key to that code is somewhere in this room. The key must be a book, hidden amongst these other books."

"But which book?" I asked aridly. "There are quite a few here."

Holmes' eyes scanned the shelves. "Fitzroy would want to keep it in a place that shouldn't arouse suspicion. A book cast about on the floor would be the first to be searched. The bookshelf seems the most likely hiding spot then."

Holmes proceeded to pluck a few volumes from the shelf with his long, dexterous fingers. "It would a well-thumbed volume," he said more to himself than to me, "no doubt held open for long periods of time as he wrote his messages. A book with a creased spine and broken binding seems, then, most likely."

At length his fingers stopped over the spin of a hefty volume which he pulled down. Glancing at the cover, I knew Holmes to have found the right one: *The Legend of the Golem and Other Tales of Ancient Prague*.

"Well," I said, "we have the key but –"

Before I could finish, Holmes had opened the book and a few loose sheets fell from its pages. I stooped to pick them up and read the hastily-drafted message written thereon:

Should this message be found, then surely I am dead. It is an eventuality that I foresaw. What I regrettably cannot foresee is who shall find this message. If you are one of the perpetrators of this plot, then everything I have to say shall be familiar to you. Should you be one of His Majesty's men enlisted to find me, then I can only hope that this shall prove helpful to you. I speak now not in riddles and in code for, beyond grave, I am beyond being in danger.

Not everyone, I have discovered, has approved of the unification of the German kingdoms of Bohemia and Moravia. The formation of Czechoslovakia has incited dangerous nationalism in quarters of the country, and there are some who have gone so far as to plot separation. These groups have, since the unification, remained dormant, but I fear that one of them is plotting for something much grander. My gathered intelligence suggests that this group is plotting to bomb Wenceslas Square, the great boulevard of this city, and this action shall only be the first in a series of calamitous occurrences which are designed to weaken the city of Prague. From there, splinter groups throughout the county shall carry on this deadly plot, crippling Czechoslovakia in revenge for their unification.

I hope that I am still alive on 25 June when this deadly action shall commence, but I fear that my time is running short. Should you be on my fellow King's men, I trust that you shall do with this information what you will. Report it to the proper authorities and prevent tragedy from befalling this beautiful new country. If you are my enemy, take solace in the knowledge that you have eliminated me. But know that your secrets have been exposed. I went to my grave knowing the full truth of your devilish plot, and I sincerely hope that others out there will take up my work and quash your plans.

God Save the King,

G. Fitzroy – 1919

Holmes and I stood in silence reading and re-reading Fitzroy's last words. At length, he set the paper aside and drew in a deep breath.

"What do we do?" I asked.

"Though I am loath to do so," Holmes said after a moment of consideration, "I think it best that we do as Fitzroy says: 'report it to the proper authorities.' We have luckily made the acquaintance, and I daresay an impression, upon the good Inspector Horák. We had best come clean about our true involvement in this matter. He is made of more manpower than we, my dear fellow, and they can be put to good use especially since Fitzroy claims this deadly action is only twenty-four hours from now."

Holmes stopped and considered for a moment more. "However," he added, "I should think that our part in this has not come to an end. There is still one principle player that we have not yet encountered, and I should very much like to meet him."

"And who is that?" I said.

"Someone I rather think shall warrant the use of your service revolver," Holmes said grimly. "I speak, of course, of the Golem."

IV

I consulted my watch and saw that it was gone nine o'clock of the following evening and, despite the fact that Holmes and I had been out-of-doors all day, I was beginning to feel pent up. We had paced the length of Wenceslas Square more times than I could count throughout the day, both of us keeping our eyes open for any suspicious activity. I did my part not to make eye contact with Inspector Horák's plain-clothed men who had sat at café tables for much of the day doing just as we were.

It had been a tumultuous day since we had located Fitzroy's hiding place and discovered the nature of the plot he had uncovered. We did as Holmes had suggested and delivered Fitzroy's letter into the hands of the Inspector at his office. The Inspector gave us a knowing smile as we entered his rooms, plucking the pipe from his mouth and standing to greet us. "When Mr. Sherlock Holmes is to be found in your city," he said, "one should know that he is there on official business."

We had given him Fitzroy's correspondence and the Inspector immediately jumped into action, designating tasks to his officers and preparing for the day-long vigil that we now all undertook. For hours which masqueraded as a lifetime, we watched the comings-and-goings of the city, kept an eye out as people disembarked the electric tram cars that ran through the square, and acquainted ourselves with the countenances of those men and women who seemed to linger just a little too long in one spot. More than once, I pressed the cold steel of my revolver into my breast as my hand closed around it, but it was for naught.

And now, as the sun had disappeared beneath the city sky, I felt even more on edge. The crowds in the square had dwindled, but those who did pass through were luxuriously dressed, no doubt on their way to a night at the theatre or returning from a sumptuous dinner somewhere else in the city. I suddenly had the strangest feeling deep in my breast that something was amiss and if any attack were to take place, it would be now.

No sooner had this curious pang welled up inside of me, did Holmes suddenly reach out and grasp hold of my arm, subtlety pointing in the direction of a tall, lean man who was disembarking from a tramcar dressed in a mackintosh with a dark trilby pulled low over his eyes. Tucked under his arm was a package wrapped in brown paper and tied with a length of twine. To the untrained eye one would not have suspected anything, but Holmes and I were certain that that was our man. I had the sudden urge to rush forward and subdue him at once, but Holmes held me back, no doubt reading the compulsion in my eyes.

"Steady yourself, man," he hissed. "Wait for it."

Our man approached a bench and took a seat, nervously crossing and uncrossing his ankles. He removed a watch from his pocket and checked the time before stowing it away again. Then, setting the package down gingerly upon the bench, he stood and hastily began to cross the square.

"Now, Watson," said Holmes, rushing forward. "Now!"

From his inner pocket, Holmes withdrew a police whistle and touching it to his lips he let out one long, shrill blast. The man cast an anxious look over his shoulder and then broke out into an all-out run. By this time, three officers had approached us. Holmes gestured towards the package left upon the bench and then, after cautioning the men to its deadly contents, grabbed me by the arm and pulled me away from the throng and after our man. For an instant I was conscious of a moment of extreme clarity which could not understand how I had done so much running in two days' time. Surely, I reasoned, this was the work of a much younger man, and not a man entering his dotage. If Sherlock Holmes showed any strain upon his constitution, however, he did not show it, for he was already ahead of me, closing the gap between us and our man.

We had gradually been running uphill and, coming to the top of the hill, we watched our man flee down a side street.

No longer surrounded by the crowds in the square, I pulled my revolver from my pocket and prepared to aim and fire in an effort to wound our man and quell his attempts at escape, but Holmes stopped me.

"Think what other tricks he may have up his sleeve," he said. "We cannot risk it."

Then he was off again, sprinting after the man, all the while clutching his silver-headed stick in hand. I rushed to follow, the now all-to-familiar burning sensation returning to plague my lungs. We had entered the mouth of the side street down which our man had flown, but he suddenly appeared to have vanished. Holmes and I stopped, looking about us for any sign of him, but our attention was arrested by the sound of a man's voice from very nearby:

"You may have foiled my plans," he said in a heavily German-accented voice, "but for that you shall escape this street alive."

Then, out of a pool of shadows, our man stepped and stopped before us, a malign smile upon his face. I leveled my revolver at him and pulled back the hammer, but I was suddenly stopped by a sight that I could not fathom.

Out of the same inky darkness stepped another figure that I took at first not to be human. Indeed, even as my eyes became accustomed to the mountain of a man before me, I could not believe my eyes. The thing that stood before us must have been at least seven feet in height and broad all over; his massive shoulders and arms easily the thickness of an uprooted tree. He was barefoot and dressed in little more than a simple white cloth, for I could not think how such a beast could find clothes that would fit its immense frame. But it was the beast's visage – somehow not entirely human – which chilled me even more to the core. I stood transfixed, my unbelieving eyes simply not comprehending the thing that stood before us, the thing that had lurched out of the night at us, and it was a feat in itself to pry my gaze from the beast – the Golem – and cast a glance at Holmes who stood just as rooted to the spot as I, and who looked on in sheer terror.

I must have steeled up enough courage, however, to take aim at the beast before us and fire, but my hand was unsteady and my shot was wide, embedding itself in the stonework of the alleyway which closed in around us and trapped us with the thing that would surely mean our deaths in time. The shot must have angered the creature, for the

Golem lumbered towards me even as I attempted to fire again. My sweaty fingers slipped over the trigger and suddenly the revolver had fallen from my grasp. I contemplated clambering for it on the ground, when I felt a great hand upon my neck and then the horrible feeling of air beneath my feet. The Golem had hoisted me up from the ground, and I felt its grip on the back of my throat begin to tighten. This was how it was to end; I contemplated, with my life squeezed out of me by a thing not truly human in this back alley. I tried to flail and kick my way out, but my body was failing me.

And then, from the corner of my eye I caught sight of Sherlock Holmes as he wildly swung his cane over his head. Its silver handle made contact with the Golem's ribs and I swore that I heard the beast let out a groan of pain. Its grip on my neck loosened ever so slightly, and I began to wriggle my way out of its harsh grasp. Holmes swung his cane again and I took this chance to muster up what little energy I had and deliver a powerful blow with the back of my heel to the creature's stomach. The Golem let out another cry and dropped me entirely. I made hard contact with the ground and, though winded, I had enough wherewithal to run my hands over the cobbles and land upon my revolver. Turning over onto my back, I saw Holmes with his stick raised over his head once more face-to-face with the Golem, holding the creature at bay as best he could. I pulled back the hammer of the revolver, listened to its satisfying click, and then squeezed off a shot.

The Golem clasped a massive hand to its own throat and then, like a felled tree, toppled to the ground dead.

Sherlock Holmes had little time to celebrate such a victory, however, for he was already looking for our other man, but it seemed as if he had used our struggle with the beast as an opportunity to take to his heels and flee. Dejection evident on his face, Holmes helped me to his feet.

"You needn't worry about it," I panted breathlessly. "You got a good enough look at him. And if you did not, then I certainly did. We can supply Horák with as much information as he needs."

"You are, of course, right, my dear fellow," Holmes said, clapping me upon the shoulder. "If there is one thing that we can take away from this little adventure of ours, it is that sometimes the combined forces of Sherlock Holmes and Dr. Watson are not enough. Occasionally we need the outside help of others."

I turned my attention to the behemoth that lay prostrate at our feet, my eyes traveling to the still-warm gun in my hands. For an instant, my mind clouded in confusion. Could the thing really have been the Golem – the creature born out of clay so many centuries earlier? Surely not, and yet, I was inclined to believe almost anything when I had felt its great grip on the back of my neck. Sherlock Holmes, seemingly always able to divine my thoughts, regarded me with a bemused grin.

"This is not the storied creature that we have heard so much about of late," he said. "Look upon his visage now, Watson, and you shall see what tricks the mind may play upon you."

I did as my friend said and saw that, although the dead man was hardly handsome, there wasn't anything particularly remarkable about his appearance at all. Indeed, it had been my mind playing tricks on me in the low light of that alleyway that had conjured up the demonic countenance that had so terrified me. I almost felt like laughing.

"It is a face I do believe I recognize," Holmes added. "I should have known earlier. Had I divined the link between the Golem and the radicals sooner than I did, all would have fallen into place. In my researches I have more than once come across the name Klaus Schneider, commonly known in some circles as 'The Goliath' or 'The Golem.' If a foreign element was to be involved in this business, and there were reported sightings of a creature believed to be the legendary Golem, then Schneider's ought to have been a name on my mind from the start. Luckily, we have brought an end to the Golem's reign of terror once and for all."

Two days later we found ourselves once more in a train compartment trundling across the continent. We had spent the intervening time clearing up loose ends with Inspector Horák and, from our description of our man, it sounded as though finding him should hardly be a challenge. Indeed, as we packed our things for our return trip, we received word from Horák that he was in police custody.

Holmes was in a communicative mood as our train drew out of Czechoslovakia, and he was happily discussing the case:

"I really should have been more on the trail sooner, my dear fellow. Should you ever find reason to draw up this case for your records – a personal account, only, for Mycroft should never let such a tale reach the public – then you really must put it down as one of my failures. My suspicions ought to have been aroused as soon as Palan told us that he knew nothing of what happened to Fitzroy. If someone in the Czech underworld had been responsible then some whisper of the business would surely have made its way back to him. However, since it was a ring of German radicals responsible for this plot, then it stood to reason that Palan should have been totally unaware."

"I just thank god that we were not too late," I said. "When we discovered Fitzroy's letter, we had only twenty-four hours' time to foil the plot. Imagine if we had even been one day later."

"From time to time," Sherlock Holmes said, "I am inclined to believe in the hand of Fate. These past few days have been one of those times, and fortunately for us, Fate appears to have been on our side."

Holmes cast a glance out of the train window.

"It is a changing world, my dear Watson," he mused quietly, "and we have played our small part in facilitating that change. With luck that change is for the better. Only time shall tell, Watson. For us. For Czechoslovakia. For the world. Only time shall tell."

In the Footsteps of Madness

"It must be no less than murder," said Sherlock Holmes as he stared out of the window. Wind and rain lashed at the panes and with night having fallen on the city, London had taken on an even more ominous aspect than usual. I sat in the warm glow of the fire, a cognac in one hand, the latest edition of *The Times* in the other and, at my friend's startling exclamation, I looked up in some surprise.

"I perceive the familiar figure of Inspector Bradstreet making his way towards out flat," Holmes said by way of an explanation. "I have never known Bradstreet to be particularly fleet of foot and, why he simply wouldn't have taken a cab here – especially when one considers the foul state of the weather – I should wager that whatever brings him in our direction has caused him some great duress. And, the Inspector having chosen to come on foot suggests that whatever it is happened very recently too."

I thought I detected the ghost of a smile cross Holmes' face. There was nothing like the beginning of some new mystery to pique his curiosity.

"You will of course stay, Doctor, to hear the Inspector's case through?"

"I wouldn't miss it for the world," I replied.

Holmes laughed aloud and opened the door to our sitting room wide; calling down to Mrs. Hudson to admit the Inspector as soon as he arrived on our doorstep.

Though it was Sherlock Holmes who derived the most pleasure from the commencement of a new case, I confess that I too found the thrill exhilarating. It had only been a matter of weeks since Holmes and I had returned from Dartmoor where we had investigated the business involving Sir Henry Baskerville; a case which I shall long remember as surely one of the strangest and darkest which my friend and I had ever investigated. The time which had elapsed since the conclusion of that affair had passed by slowly. They were filled with interesting problems, but none had held Holmes the way that the Baskerville case had, and I daresay that we both hoped that whatever Inspector Bradstreet was bringing us would perhaps be the beginning of something big once again.

The Inspector, a tall, stout official, arrived in our sitting room harried and thoroughly soaked to the skin. He was short of breath and, after I had pressed a glass of brandy into his hand which he downed quickly, he took a seat on the settee in an effort to regain his composure. At length he said:

"I have just come from the scene of the strangest business which I have ever seen, Mr. Holmes."

Holmes settled into his own chair before the fire, and crossed one long leg over the other as he pressed his fingertips together in his usual method of contemplation. "Pray, lay all of the facts before me, Inspector, and omit nothing."

Bradstreet drew in a deep breath. "It's murder, Mr. Holmes. The most ghastly that I have ever clapped eyes on. You are doubtlessly aware, sir, that construction is being done to the city sewer system across the Thames in Battersea. Construction has been underway for nearly three weeks and there have been no major incidents reported by any of the workers. That was, until, last evening when one man, John Kelly, disappeared while working on a newly excavated portion of the line. It was no surprise to any of the other men that Kelly did not keep to their routine. He was a hard-working man, they said, determined to support the young wife and child that he had at home. However, when almost a day had elapsed and Kelly was not heard from, the men decided to concentrate their efforts on finding their missing comrade. They were not searching long before he was found."

Bradstreet – one of the most stalwart of the Scotland Yard men who came to our door for assistance – drew in another deep breath. The faintest shiver passed through me. Whatever it was that had frightened the man so must have been a spectacle indeed to chill the blood in Bradstreet's veins.

"There was hardly anything left of Kelly when he was discovered," Bradstreet said choosing his words with care. "The man had been savaged – as though he'd been attacked by some ferocious animal. I made an examination of the body in the city morgue. I can attest to the savagery with which he was killed. It was simply inhuman. And if it was a man who did it to Kelly, I would surely not wish to make his acquaintance."

"What leads have you followed thus far, Inspector?"

"I have tried to learn as best I could what John Kelly did in the last moments before his death."

From his inner breast pocket, Bradstreet withdrew a small notebook. "Two nights ago, according to his wife, he returned home in a pleasant mood. He spent the night at home – as he usually did. Mrs. Kelly attested to the hard work which her husband did throughout the day, and how he liked nothing more to come at night and spend an evening by the fire reading a book or the paper. On the morning of his death, Kelly awoke, dressed and headed to work early. He was seen by one of his fellow construction workers – a man named William McGoven. McGoven said that he exchanged a few pleasant words with Kelly before Kelly decided to descend into the freshly-dug excavation site and begin work.

"That was the last time that anyone saw John Kelly alive on this earth."

I could almost see the cogs turning in Sherlock Holmes' brain from behind his closed eyes. At length, he opened them and said, "Your case interests me a great deal, Bradstreet. Fortunately, I have been singularly unoccupied of late and can devote my full attentions to the matter."

The Scotland Yard man sighed visibly in relief. "What do you propose to do first?"

"I must see the body of the late John Kelly," Holmes replied. "If the wounds which resulted in Kelly's death is really as ghastly as you make them out to be than I believe that they shall be most instructive as well."

So saying, Holmes jumped up from his seat and made for his room, emerging a moment later shrugging on his frock coat.

"You intend to go now," I asked, observing my watch and noting that it was very nearly ten.

"There is no time like the present, Watson," Holmes replied, reaching for his hat and stick. "The game is very much afoot and I want to get a start while the scent is still fresh. Would you wish to accompany the Inspector and me?"

Once more I told Holmes that I would not miss another exercise of his brilliant cognitive abilities for the world, and after I had shuffled out of my slippers and thrown on my coat and hat as well, the three of us descended the seventeen steps from our sitting room to the foyer, and made our way out into the deluge. Holmes hailed a passing four-wheeler and once we had piled inside, Bradstreet called out to the cabbie to take us to the morgue. It was a solemn ride carried out much in silence as we rattled through the pouring rain in the middle of the night. The glow of a passing gas lamp gave a shiny luster to the ancient cobbles over which we now rode, but I have seldom remembered London ever looking so grey and foreboding as it did that night.

In due course, our cab eased to a stop outside of a plain-looking stone building and we alighted. The room into which we entered was low and dim; a few lamps and candles were scattered throughout the room, but they did nothing to make it feel more welcoming. The smell of death lingered long in the air and, though I have spent the better part of my life in the medical profession, I still found the stench a strong and unpleasant one. The mortuary attendant on duty nodded his head at Bradstreet as we entered, and his face too became drawn of color.

"I reckon I know what you've come about, sir," the attendant said to the Inspector. He led our group towards the back of the room where we faced a low, wooden table; the familiar shape of a human body lying on top of it covered in a once white cloth which had now been stained crimson with blood. Bradstreet nodded gravely and the attendant drew back the sheet to reveal what was left of Mr. John Kelly.

I have seen much carnage in my time, but seldom have I seen something so stomach-turning as the mutilated remains of John Kelly. The dead man had been savagely attacked: his throat torn out and his abdomen showing signs of having been viscously worried as well. Both Bradstreet and the attendant took a step back as the body was revealed, and I too found myself clasping the back of my hand to my mouth in a moment of utter surprise. Sherlock Holmes, however, seemed unmoved by the butchery before him. With his usual penetrating gaze, he inspected the body minutely with the naked eye before he inspected the wounds with even more care through his convex lens.

"Could you please turn the body over?"

The attendant did so with hesitation, and I saw that Kelly's back revealed scores of similar wounds. Holmes thanked the man and the body was returned to its position on the slab, the cloth drawn up over it once more.

"Well, Mr. Holmes," said Bradstreet pressingly.

"I should wager that your suspicions were correct, Inspector," Holmes said. "No mere mortal could have done this to Kelly. While it would certainly be singular for a human to kill in such a frenzy – though not unheard of – there are distinct signs that some of these wounds were made with teeth. A pair of what I should warrant to be enlarged, sharp canines to be more precise."

"What kind of animal could have done a thing like that?" Bradstreet asked.

"I cannot answer that question yet, I'm afraid, Inspector, but I believe I can in time. I need an opportunity to consult some reference materials. Fortunately, I have a small selection of zoological tomes back at Baker Street. I intimate a careful study of those shall fill my hours this evening."

I wanted to protest and assure Holmes that he needed his sleep, but I knew his methods all too well by now.

"There is little more that you can do now, Bradstreet," Holmes continued. "I would advise that you return home and try to get some well-needed rest."

"I don't think that I shall ever sleep again after what I have seen this night," Bradstreet replied.

I found myself mirroring the Inspector's sentiments once Holmes and I returned to 221b Baker Street that night. Though I was perfectly willing to stay up nursing another drink before the fire, Holmes asked me if I might leave him in peace.

"It is not out of the question that this shall develop into a two-pipe problem," Holmes said as he pulled a number of weathered-looking volumes from his bookshelf, "and I would not think of subjecting you to a number of hours of breathing strong shag tobacco."

I made my way to my room and sat upon my bed and stared listlessly at the wall. Sleep, I knew, what not come easily to me that night.

When sleep did finally come it was in the early hours of the morning and I found myself waking late. After I washed, and dressed, I entered our sitting room only to find that Holmes had already gone. I was informed by Mrs. Hudson that he had gone out early that morning and had refused breakfast. Despite the horrors which I had seen the night before, I found myself attacking my repast. Once I had eaten to my contentment, I tried to busy myself about the room while Holmes was away, but my mind continued to linger on the horrible death of John Kelly. I found myself perusing one of the books which Holmes had taken down the night before, but for all of my searching through its text, I couldn't find anything which seemed to be of use to us.

It was nearing noon when Holmes at last returned. He seemed to be a satisfied mood; an ever-so-slight spring in his step as he hung up his hat. "I believe that I am on the right track, Watson," he said as he took his usual seat.

"I know how you like to keep your suppositions to yourself," I said lighting a cigarette, "but I must know what progress you have made. For the life of me, I am baffled."

Holmes too lighted a cigarette and leaned back in his chair. "I have endeavored to teach you many things, Doctor," he said with some condescension, "but it appears as though I have much more to teach you yet. The facts of the case seem to me to be quite simple."

Holmes reached for one of the zoological reference books. Flipping through its pages, he stopped and pushed the open book towards me. "This chapter," he said, "concentrates on the big cats of the Asian continent. I found it quite interesting reading especially after I noticed that a number of the wounds which killed John Kelly were inflicted by large canines. While this did not necessarily narrow down the list of animals which could have killed Kelly, I knew that I was in search of a mammal. The more I inspected the corpse, the more I became convinced that the animal was a large cat; either a lion or a tiger. You will recall that I asked the attendant to turn the body over so I could inspect the back. It was then that I noticed the deep cuts on either sides of Kelly's lower back which had been dealt by sharp claws. This manner of attack is common among tigers."

To illustrate his point, Holmes flipped the page in the book and pointed with a long, bony finger at an illustration of a tiger pouncing upon the back of a running gazelle.

"A tiger?" I asked, my brain still processing the incredible train of logic.

"Yes, a tiger," Holmes retorted coldly. "In this instance, even the most seemingly abstruse of situations can become elementary when properly analyzed."

"Well," I said, "with this profoundly unusual information in hand, what did you do about it this morning?"

"I set off to speak to the management of the largest zoos in the city of London," Holmes replied. "It was quite a task. Most of the gentlemen with whom I spoke were rather reluctant to speak to me. But only one was *afraid*. It was he, Watson, who informed me that one week ago, a tiger broke free while it was being transported from one cage to another. Though the zookeepers did their utmost to track the beast down and re-capture it, their search proved unsuccessful.

"As I see it, this tiger, having broken out of its confines, makes a break for the Thames and perhaps attempts to sustain itself feeding off of the fishes in the river. Invariably, it will find its way into one of the sewer drain pipes which flows into the Thames and, from there, the animal found itself in the sewer system proper where it eventually crossed paths with the unfortunate John Kelly who just so happened to be in the wrong place at the most inconvenient of times."

"That is quite extraordinary," I replied. "But…whatever can we do now?"

From his inner pocket, Holmes withdrew a small glass bottle and tossed it to me. "That," he said, "is a fur sample from the animal's old cage. Providing it to me was, of course, the least that the zookeeper could do for me, and he happily supplied it when asked."

Holmes crushed his cigarette into the ashtray at his side and then closed the heavy book with a *thud* to emphasize his point. "This evening," he said, "I will give that fur sample to the one companion that I would rather have at my side than an entire fleet of Scotland Yard men and he shall lead me directly to that tiger."

"Toby!" I cried enthusiastically.

"Precisely! Toby and I shall seek out that animal this night so it cannot possibly do any more harm than it has already done."

"I must come with you," I said. "Going alone is going to your certain doom, Holmes. I cannot stand idly by."

A smile played upon Holmes' habitually cruel mouth. "My many thanks, Watson. Your willingness to risk yourself at my side is always appreciated. However, if you are to accompany me, than I must insist that you drop your service revolver into your pocket. I shall be doing much the same. I speak quite literally when I say that we are headed into the lion's den."

We traveled by cab once night had begun to fall to Number 3 Pinchin Lane, the home of Holmes' curious friend, Sherman, the owner of a veritable menagerie, where we collected the dog, Toby. It had been some time since I had clapped eyes upon the creature; not since the strange affair of Jonathan Small, the one-legged man, and his deadly accomplice had Holmes and I employed Toby's remarkable tracking skills. I confess that it was an uncomfortable ride by carriage with the animal seated across both Holmes' lap and my own as we trundled through the night towards the excavation site which had been the place of John Kelly's unfortunate demise.

Alighting, Holmes took the small bottle of fur from his inner pocket, opened it, and wafted it under Toby's nose. The dog sniffed and then took off suddenly leaving Holmes and myself to lurch after it. We descended quickly into the excavation site, a process which was much easier said than done. Toby had no issue traversing the muddy decline into the bowels of the earth, but Holmes and I found it more difficult to keep our firm footing. My friend especially had to pull to Toby's leash on more than one occasion so as to not fall face-first into the ground.

Once we reached the bottom of the hill and had found ourselves into the sewers proper, it was easier to keep control of Toby. He continued, hot on the scent, as we dutifully followed. Holmes had had the forethought to bring with us a bulls-eye lantern which he had pressed into my hand. Lighting it and opening the shutter, I illuminated our path through the labyrinth-like system. All the while, I kept a firm hand on my coat pocket, pressing the cold, dead steel of my service revolver into my chest; reassured by its presence so close to my breast. If we did find the animal that had killed Kelly this night, I thought to myself, it would be best that I remained on my guard.

For how long we walked through the empty sewers, and how far we marched, I cannot say. However, a great deal of time had elapsed, and I was beginning to suspect that we were walking aimlessly in circles. I mentioned as much to Holmes.

"That is precisely what is happening, Watson," Holmes countered with some irritation. "I fear that Toby has lost the scent."

"Ought you to give him another whiff of that fur sample?" I asked.

Holmes shook his head with contempt. "No," he replied, defeat clouding his voice, "there is always the possibility that the escaped tiger did wonder aimlessly like we are now, but I fear that there are simply too many conflicting variables here. It was a long-shot that Toby would be able to track the beast down to begin with. If you are an honest man, Watson, you shall set this down as one my failures and show to the world what a fool I truly can be."

"What should we do then?" I asked.

"I'm afraid there is little that we can do beyond returning Toby to old Sherman, and making our way back to Baker Street to ruminate on my hubris. Tomorrow morning, I shall send a telegram to Bradstreet informing him of the progress that we have made and perhaps then he can arrange a number of officers to descend down here and find the creature together."

Holmes pulled at my arm as he spun Toby around and endeavored to find the way back. How far afield we were from our point of origin, I could only speculate, but we soon found ourselves in what I took to be familiar environs; the distant sound of the outside world distant as they came down through the excavation site. Holmes and I were in the process of rounding a corner from one tunnel to the next when we caught sight of something standing out far from where we stood.

At first glance, what we perceived was the figure of a tall, broad man who was standing with his legs spread apart; long, thick arms dangling at his sides. Who he was and what he was doing here, I had no time to wonder before he seemed to sense our presence and turn on us suddenly.

Never in the delirious ravings of a disordered brain could anything more shocking, and terrifying than the creature that confronted us be imagined. Though the shape appeared to be a man, both Holmes and I perceived at once that the man's features were not those of a human being, but surely the visage of some big cat; perhaps not unlike the tiger we had both sought. Yet I knew at once that this monstrosity was not the tiger that we were chasing. This *thing* was something else entirely.

In the low light of the bulls-eye lantern, I caught a glimpse of two large, yellow eyes which blazed with hot intensity. I noted too that the thing was not clothed, but its body was covered in thick fur. I felt a sudden wave of nausea mixed with intense fear cloud my judgment before the thing opened its mouth to reveal two immense fangs, and with a two powerful bounds, the thing was upon us.

Neither Holmes nor I had time to react to the creature's attack. I was only beginning to reach for my revolver when I felt a clawed hand tear through my coat, and with incredible strength, I was lifted off of my feet and thrown background at least one foot. I landed on my back in a pool of shallow water. I had had the wind knocked out of me, and I was dizzy from both the tumble and sheer fright. Sputtering wildly, I looked up in time to see the creature turn his attentions towards

Holmes. Time seemed to crawl to a standstill as the thing raised the same clawed hand with the intent to do much the same as it did to me to the detective. I saw that my friend was transfixed by the creature; seemingly hypnotized by its impossible presence here in the sewer. I vaguely recall calling out to Holmes; my voice seeming to come from some distant place, unable to contend with the ringing in my head. My cry seemed to break Holmes from his reverie, and he too reached for his own firearm, as the creature swatted it from his grip.

I watched in terror as Holmes, now defenseless against the great beast, was cornered against the stone wall. Suddenly, Toby, leaping from the ground, latched onto the creature's forearm; sinking his own canines into the great tree-trunk-like triceps of the monster. The beast, in turn, unleashed a guttural snarl, and attempted to pluck the dog from its arm. Fearing now just as much for the well-being of the dog, I managed to pull myself up onto my side, and reached for my revolver. Whipping it from my pocket, I hurriedly pulled back the hammer, and did not hesitate and squeezing off three shots in quick succession. Each hit their mark in the creature's flank, and it went limp suddenly; crumbling like a wilting flower.

Toby let go of the creature's arm and it pressed a paw to its wounds, staggering away.

Holmes and I locked eyes and we both knew that the nightmarish vision was mortal. He too reached for his own revolver and fired off a round at the retreating beast. It squealed in agony as it went down, falling first to its knees and then tumbling forward face-first into the briny water.

The thing was dead.

Holmes and I both heaved a collective sigh of relief.

"You are unhurt?" I asked Holmes.

"I am fine," he said, "but I really should be asking you, old friend."

"I'm fine," I said, pressing a hand to the wound on my stomach. I looked down and saw that the creature's claws had succeeded in tearing through both my coat and waistcoat, and had drawn blood beneath. But, it appeared as though the wound was superficial; a mere scratch. There were, I believed, more important matters to address. "What in god's name was that thing?"

I lifted the bulls-eye lantern and held it aloft over the thing's corpse. At first glance, I would have taken the beast to be a Neanderthal; some specimen of Neolithic man which had not evolved through the centuries. But, the thick fur and the cat-like features which were now surely engrained in my mind, spoke to something far deeper than a missing link.

"For once in my life," Sherlock Holmes said, "I am completely and utterly lost. What that *thing* is, I cannot say at all."

Holmes knelt down and I pushed the lamplight closer towards the body. "The specimen is a perfect one," Holmes continued. "Looking at the arm, one can detect a history of surgery being performed on the creature. You will note, Watson, there are scars – the tell-tale sign of the knife – which had begun to heal."

"You mean to say that this was the result of some crude laboratory experiment?" I asked.

"So it would seem," Holmes replied grimly. "This creature is no natural being. And look here, at the hands."

I shone the lamplight towards the claws which had inflicted their mark upon me. "The fingers," said Holmes, "are incomplete. You can see where the paws of a creature – perhaps a tiger or a panther – still began. I am sure of it, Watson; this thing was born on the operating table."

Again, a wave of nausea overtook me. "Who could have possibly done such a monstrous thing?"

"I have not the slightest idea," Holmes replied. "However, seeing how this beast reacted to both you and me, I am now sure that it was responsible for the death of John Kelly and not the escaped tiger as I formerly suspected."

Holmes stood and I endeavored to do so as well, wincing against the cuts across my stomach.

"Are you sure that you are unhurt, Watson?"

"I'm fine," I said. I was still very much trying to come to grips with the reality of this impossible scenario. "What do you intend to do next?"

"I will tend to Toby. And then I must utilize his nose once again. I must find out where this creature came from – even if it's just some idea. As for you, old man, I am sending you back to Baker Street. I cannot, in good conscience, embark upon another hike with you in the condition you're in. I would recommend a few bandages and a stiff drink to calm your nerves. I doubt that either of us will ever forget what we have seen here tonight."

It was not without much protest that I eventually left Holmes, who I last saw kneeling down before Toby, scratching the dog behind its ears. I found my way out of the chasm and was able to hail a cab; the driver surely perturbed by his fare's disheveled appearance and disbelieving countenance. As the hansom conveyed me homeward, the events which had transpired earlier played out in my head once more: each second was now etched into my memory and chilled the blood in my veins. I arrived at Baker Street and was happy to find that Mrs. Hudson had already retired for I did not wish to disturb her with tales of the grim events of the night. I made my way up to our rooms where I cleaned my scratches, and laid my torn clothes upon the bed thinking how my tailor would have wept should he have seen the state of my suit. I then settled into the sitting room and poured myself a drink endeavoring to wait up until Holmes' return.

The hours crawled by and, though I have spent many nights in a sleepless vigil, I daresay that that was one of the longest. It was nigh three in the morning by the time Sherlock Holmes returned, he too looking a little worse for wear. While he was fortunate to have sustained no injury during the contretemps in the sewers, he looked exhausted and his clothes were stained and battered speaking to arduous hours' work since we parted ways. Once I had pushed a drink into my companion's hand, and he had slipped into his dressing gown, I pressed him for details.

"You will be glad to learn, Watson," Holmes began, "that nothing as dramatic as what you experienced happened to me once we parted ways. As I had hoped, though, Toby was still game for another jaunt. Having him smell the creature which lay dead before us, we took off in what I perceived to be a north-easterly direction; a hypothesis I confirmed when we stopped and I clambered through a manhole to get my bearings. I did this no less than half-a-dozen times in the short time that was to follow, and eventually Toby and I found ourselves only a stones-throw from the Thames itself. We climbed out onto the street and much to my surprise – and my gratification – Toby managed to pick up the scent again, and we went off once more.

"In short order, we came upon a row of warehouses along the Thames: each one a decrepit reminder of the days of yore. Each building, a twisted, mangled wreck of broken windows and falling bricks, seemed to stand unoccupied, but Toby pressed on, his determined nose to the pavement. Minding the broken glass which was scattered across the ground, we eventually came upon a building before which

Toby stopped as though he'd found the origin point of the smell. I managed to climb through one of the broken windows and into the building proper and was confused to find that it was completely empty. There was no sign of life inhabiting that place for some time.

"The building was not without some points of interest, mind you. There were obvious signs that whoever had once inhabited the place had vacated the premises quickly. And, in no less than seven places, I perceived distinct splotches of some chemical agent upon the floor. The stains were far too old to speak with any precise accuracy as to the exact nature of those chemicals, but it was simplicity itself to render a hypothesis from it all."

"You'd stumbled across the laboratory where that *thing* was created," I said.

"Exactly," Holmes replied. "However, with little else to draw upon, I determined that it was time to return Toby and, after rudely rousing Sherman from his slumber, returned to you. Yet, I think it would be a lie to suggest that my brain has been idle since then."

"Oh? How do you mean?"

"I began to cast my mind back to some years ago when I happened to chance upon a curious article in one of the more lurid newspapers. It spoke to a certain scandal which had erupted out of one of the smaller London universities of the sciences concerning one of their preeminent physiologists – a man called Moreau."

"I remember that article!" I cried. "The news broke just around the time that I graduated from the University of London before I entered the army. Was not this Dr. Moreau charged with crimes pertaining to the cruelty of animals after performing experiments involving *vivisection?*"

"You have hit upon it, Watson," Holmes said slapping his knee with pride. "Following the scandal, Moreau obviously found London too hot to hold him and we fled the city. He has not been heard from again since. Nonetheless, in the wake of his disappearance, some of Moreau's fellow scientists began to emerge from the woodwork speaking to his crackpot theories. It appears as though Dr. Moreau had some delusions of grandeur and hoped to play God, creating man out of his animal brethren."

"Then surely," I said, "the creature that we happened upon was a result of Moreau's work."

"If only the truth were so simple," Holmes responded grimly. "The creature that we encountered was quite young. From a cursory examination of its teeth and body, I was able to ascertain an age of approximately six months. Dr. Moreau has been out of London for at least nine years. That leaves us with only one explanation, I'm afraid."

"Someone is continuing Moreau's work," I said.

"Yes," Holmes murmured, the thought perhaps too horrific to fully contemplate. "We must begin to seek out the man who is now following in the footsteps of Dr. Moreau."

I hardly slept a wink that night. A myriad of ghastly thoughts floated in and out of my brain, each one featured some new haunting visage which screamed in my mind's eye. I awoke the next morning in a cold sweat. After washing and redressing the bandages which I had applied to my wounds, I joined Holmes for breakfast. He greeted me warmly enough and pushed the papers towards me. I unfurled it and was surprised by the most unusual of headlines:

Police Apprehend Wild Animal in London

"Go on," Holmes said, "read it. We could both use some levity this morning."

Unfurling the rest of the page, I read through the article. 'Early this morning,' it ran, 'Inspector Lestrade of Scotland Yard led a group of fifteen constables on a most perilous of missions. Following a number of reports concerning a tiger which was glimpsed along the banks of the Thames, the representatives of the law were tasked with capturing it. According to the Inspector, the tiger has been traced back to an as yet unnamed zoo in the metropolitan area which lost their tiger nearly a week ago. The task of capturing the tiger, said the Inspector, was one which he shall never forget.'

"It seems as if we were not the only ones who encountered one of Mother Nature's most aberrant creatures last night," Holmes said with a slight smile. I managed a meager smile in response.

"What do you intend to do today?" I asked after I poured a cup of coffee.

"I awoke early this morning and sent off a telegram to the university at which Moreau was one time employed,"

Holmes replied, "and have set up a meeting with the current chair of the zoology department. The man is, curiously enough, a distant relation of mine, Watson. You shall no doubt be able to note the familial mercurial temperament."

We were soon trundling across the city towards one of the city's smallest, but most preeminent universities, whose name I shall not divulge within these pages for I should never wish to defame the reputation of such a revered academy. Holmes and I alighted and entered a large, columned building which looked as if it had stood for centuries: its Greco-Roman design lending its appearance some similarity to the ancient Parthenon. Holmes and I ascended a cramped set of stairs to the third floor of the building, and from there into a small office which was overpopulated with books. The room certainly felt too small for its only occupant: an immensely large man whose round face was hidden beneath an equally massive, dark bushy beard. Never have I seen so grandiose a figure in my life, and the man's sheer size and aura made it nigh impossible to determine his age. Upon our entering, his eyes lit up.

"Sherlock!" the man cried, "what a pleasure! You have no idea how glad I was to receive your telegram this morning."

"I wish that I could visit under circumstances, George," Holmes replied taking a seat. He gestured in my direction. "This is my friend and associate, Dr. John Watson. Watson, I would like to introduce you to my cousin, Professor George-Edward Challenger."

I shook the Professor's hand; grasped mine with an oversized appendage and held it with an iron grip.

"Now then, Sherlock," Challenger said leaning back in his chair, which I for a moment thought was to burst under his great size, "you were characteristically short on details in your correspondence. How may I be of assistance?"

"I need to know everything you have to tell me about a former employee of this department," Holmes said coldly, "one Dr. Moreau."

Even behind his great beard, I could see the Professor blanch. "We're just succeeding in putting that bad business behind us, Sherlock," he said, "why must you dredge it back up again?"

"It is a matter of murder," Holmes retorted coldly. That succeeded in seeming to prick the Professor's pomposity. "I have reason to believe that someone is following in Moreau's footsteps in some attempt to replicate his experiments. Do you know of anyone who might fit such a description?"

Challenger heaved a heavy sigh. "There were a number of students who followed Moreau's work with interest," he said. "I seem to recall that many argued that vivisection ought not to be handled as harshly as it was for there are few others way for medical science to progress in its understanding of anatomy. Yet, when Moreau fled the city – all but admitting to some wrongdoing – many of even Moreau's most ardent supporters fell off and did their utmost to distance themselves from his darkening reputation. That is all except for one."

Holmes leaned forward in his chair. "His name?"

"Roger Malquest," Challenger replied. "He has, in the past few years, begun to distance himself from our university. I don't think it was by choice, for much of the staff began to ostracize Malquest for not disavowing Moreau and his experiments. It's circumstantial evidence to be sure; Sherlock, but I can think of no man more fitting your description than he."

"If I wished to pay a visit on Malquest," Holmes said, "where might I be able to do so?"

Challenger scribbled an address onto a sheet of paper. "This is his address," Challenger said, "but I don't know what good it'll do you. He's been rather difficult to get a hold of for some time." Holmes tucked the sheet away into his breast pocket. Rising to go, he thanked the Professor.

"We must really get together for a drink sometime, Sherlock," Challenger said. "Of late I have been ruminating on a few theories which I think you would find of the utmost interest."

Holmes brushed the Professor's words off with a polite nod of the head and turned to leave. We made our way out of the building and into the belly of another hansom cab; Holmes calling out to the driver the newly obtained address.

"Challenger is a curious specimen," Holmes said as we rattled through the city. "No doubt his theories are the stuff of cheap novels. When last we spoke, he attempted to persuade me that there may still be a place on this earth where dinosaurs of a bygone age roam. Ha! Nevertheless, he proves to be useful in more than one capacity. You really must remind me to tell you, Watson, of the time that Challenger and I worked a case together. The affair of the politician, the lighthouse, and the trained cormorant is one I am not likely to forget."

Our cab drew up outside of a well-appointed-looking brick building set along a picturesque boulevard. A low, iron fence closed the house off from the road, but Holmes was unperturbed by it for he vaulted over it and rushed to the door, knocking hard upon the wood with the head of his stick. When no answer came, he rang the bell which also yielded nothing.

Without a moment's hesitation, Holmes withdrew from his inner pocket a pick and applied it to the knob. In only seconds' time, he'd managed to pick the lock and eased the door open; I was a little unnerved that someone might notice us breaking-and-entering or that one of the house's occupants might still be inside. We were greeted, however, with silence as we stepped inside.

Holmes took off at once as though he knew precisely what he was looking for. I followed lamely, and found myself in the threshold of a laboratory complete with shelves of beakers and test tubes and Bunsen burners which sat unlit. Holmes rushed for a desk which was tucked in the corner of the room, and with a careful dexterity began to page through a stack of papers.

"Make yourself useful, Watson," Holmes called, "and see if you can locate a safe."

I endeavored to do so, and in short order I managed to locate a small safe which was tucked under one of the low tables which served as a workbench. I called out to Holmes and he approached the safe and instructed for me to take his place at the desk and told me to continue to search for Malquest's papers. What I was looking for, exactly, Holmes failed to mention. As I sat down, I cast a glance over my shoulder and observed Holmes; his long, bony fingers working the dial of the safe as he endeavored to open it. At length, I heard an audible click as the safe swung open and Holmes let out an exclamation of triumph. I turned to face the detective who held a sheet of paper in hand.

"It's a deed to a piece of property," Holmes said, "and judging from the address, I would stake a great deal on it being the same warehouse which Toby and I discovered last evening."

"So Malquest has been following in Moreau's footsteps, then?" I said.

"So it would appear," Holmes replied. "And, judging by the facts to which we have been party, I would estimate that after Malquest succeeded in creating the creature that we encountered, he kept it under lock and key for some time until its escape. Once the beast had broken free from whatever cage Malquest was keeping it in, he realized what a scandal this could cause. History, it seemed was repeating itself in much the way that Moreau was caught. Malquest vacated his laboratory and, I should imagine, the city in itself too."

"You imagine there's little hope in catching him now?"

"I shall do my best," Holmes said as he turned and led me out of the room, "but I shan't expend my energies on what is surely a lost cause. Come; let us make a quick stop at the telegraph office and, from there, to Baker Street."

We did as Holmes said – my friend stopping off to send a cable – and we both found ourselves settled once more in our rooms at 221b Baker Street. It was only after we had made ourselves at home that Holmes told me his cable had been to the shipping office seeking out a man who owed him a favor in hopes that he could determine whether Malqauest had booked passage out of England. The response came a few hours later. Upon Mrs. Hudson's entrance with the cable, Holmes jumped up from his chair and zealously tore open the envelope.

"'I regret to inform you Mr. Holmes,'" he read, "'that Mr. Roger Malquest booked passage on the *H.M.S. Divine* which sailed out of London this afternoon bound for America.' Much like the madman who preceded him, Watson, Malquest is gone."

Holmes threw himself back into his chair and broodily stared at a spot on the floor. "I just wish that I could have done more," he lamented. "Who knows where Moreau and Malquest shall reappear again and continue their experiments?"

Sherlock Holmes remained in a similarly foul mood for much of the next day until the last edition of *The Times* was delivered to our door; the bad news which would have soured most men's temperaments seeming to draw Holmes from his:

H.M.S. Divine Lost at Sea – All Passengers and Crew Presumed Dead

I confess that, despite the tribulations which Holmes and I experienced while investigating the death of John Kelly which led us to uncovering the horrid work of Dr. Moreau, the specifics of that nightmare did begin to fade in time. Never could I forget being attacked by that beast in the sewers, but as I married and soon found myself immersed in domestic life, the adventures – even the most peculiar – which I shared with Sherlock Holmes were oftentimes lost in the shuffle.

I was not reminded of Dr. Moreau until one day in 1896; some seven years after Holmes and I had undertaken the case. I was once more living at Baker Street and, on a night like any other, Holmes and I were settled in before the fire in our customary seats. I was languidly flipping through one of the more sensational periodicals which arrived on our doorstep from time to time, and I was arrested by the most startling of stories that I could not help but draw Holmes' attention to.

"'One Edward Prendrick,'" I said reading from the article, "'has recently returned to London after an experience which he can only describe as the most harrowing of his life. Found adrift in the South Pacific, Prendrick, who claims to be the only survivor of the lost *Lady Vain*, says that he found himself marooned on an island inhabited by one, Dr. Moreau. Readers may recall that Dr. Moreau was involved in some scandal many years ago concerning vivisection, and according to Prendrick's tale, Moreau had managed to colonize an entire island which was inhabited by creatures of his own making: part animal and part man. Prendrick says that the creatures led a revolt against the tyrannical Moreau who tried to rule over them as a god and, in doing so, killed both Moreau and his associate, one Montgomery. Prendrick's rescuers doubted his story – and his sanity for that matter – but this writer believes otherwise.'"

I set the article down and drew in a deep breath.

"It sounds as if he succeeded in the end," I murmured. "Moreau, I mean."

"But at what cost, Watson? Man will inevitably continue to explore where he ought not and dabble in things best left alone. Those who stray too close to that rocky precipice dividing humanity and some…*higher power*…they inevitably lose their balance and fall. And the pattern, I'm afraid, shall repeat. One after the other. Each following in the footsteps of madness. But let us leave that be. Lay that article aside, my friend, and let us not dwell much longer on such matters."

Acknowledgements

Much has changed since I sat down to write the acknowledgements for *The Feats of Sherlock Holmes* back in 2018, and yet I am still very much indebted to the same few people, without whom this current book could never have happened.

I wish to thank my parents for their constant support of my writing, and for lighting the fire under me to write and work on a project even when I don't feel motivated to do so.

My utmost gratitude and love must go to Madison Niness who has supported me and my writing through every burst of inspiration and every period of writer's block.

I also wish to extend thanks to Charlie Reisman. I promised you'd be mentioned in the acknowledgements in the next one, so here you are. I cannot forget Sarah McMillan and Anthony Wojciechowsky for their support and friendship. I'm not sure that anyone enjoys "The Problem of the Slashed Portrait" as much as Anthony.

Many thanks must go out to the entire team at MX Publishing, to David Marcum for the open invitation to contribute to one of his anthologies, and Brian Belanger for the excellent design work he did on *The Feats of Sherlock Holmes* and the other books that I am privileged to be a part of.

Lastly, a debt of gratitude must be paid to the young Dr. Conan Doyle whose medical practice, not flourishing the way we would have wanted, took to writing stories and created one of the greatest fictional characters of all time. Without those stories, I would have spent a lot less time making up stories of my own.

About the Author

Nick Cardillo is the author of *The Feats of Sherlock Holmes* and several short stories that have appeared in volumes of *The MX Book of New Sherlock Holmes Stories*. Nick has also contributed to Belanger Book's *Sherlock Holmes: Adventures Beyond the Canon, The Necronomicon of Solar Pons*, and *The Meeting of the Minds: The Cases of Sherlock Holmes and Solar Pons*. A devotee of Sherlock Holmes since the age of six, Nick is also a lifelong fan of the Golden Age of Detective Fiction and Hammer Horror. He is a graduate from Susquehanna University and earned his ShD - Doctorate of Sherlockiana - from the Beacon Society in 2019.

Also from Nick Cardillo

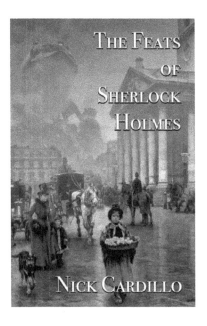

Sherlock Holmes and Dr. Watson return in six further adventures which display the great detective's brilliance once more. In these adventures set across the span of the duo's lives at 221b Baker Street, Holmes and Watson travel from the highest realms of society to the lowest dens of criminality across London in pursuit of the solution to a host of baffling mysteries. What secret does a simple wedding ring hold? What has become of a young woman fleeing the country? Can Holmes uncover the truth of a haunted house which has baffled all of London? These are but a few of the questions which shall be answered as the pages of Dr. Watson's notebooks are opened once more to reveal The Feats of Sherlock Holmes.

About MX Publishing

MX Publishing is the world's largest specialist Sherlock Holmes publisher, with over four hundred titles and two hundred authors creating the latest in Sherlock Holmes fiction and non-fiction.

Our largest project is The MX Book of New Sherlock Holmes which is the world's largest collection of new Sherlock Holmes Stories – with over two hundred contributors including NY Times bestsellers Lee Child, Nicholas Meyer, Lindsay Faye and Kareem Abdul-Jabbar. The collection has raised over $85,000 for Stepping Stones School for children with learning disabilities.

Learn more at www.mxpublishing.com

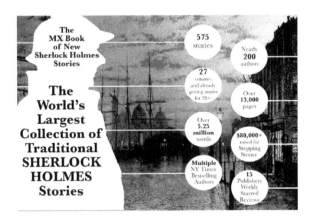

(as of May 2021 – more volumes on the way!)

Lightning Source UK Ltd.
Milton Keynes UK
UKHW021523011021
391503UK00007B/178